RUSH

JONATHAN FRIESEN

speak

An Imprint of Penguin Group (USA) Inc.

SPEAK
Published by the Penguin Group
Penguin Group (USA) Inc., 345 Hudson Street, New York, New York 10014, U.S.A.
Penguin Group (Canada), 90 Eglinton Avenue East, Suite 700, Toronto, Ontario, Canada M4P 2Y3
(a division of Pearson Penguin Canada Inc.)
Penguin Books Ltd, 80 Strand, London WC2R 0RL, England
Penguin Ireland, 25 St Stephen's Green, Dublin 2, Ireland (a division of Penguin Books Ltd)
Penguin Group (Australia), 250 Camberwell Road, Camberwell, Victoria 3124, Australia
(a division of Pearson Australia Group Pty Ltd)
Penguin Books India Pvt Ltd, 11 Community Centre, Panchsheel Park, New Delhi - 110 017, India
Penguin Group (NZ), 67 Apollo Drive, Rosedale, North Shore 0632, New Zealand
(a division of Pearson New Zealand Ltd.)
Penguin Books (South Africa) (Pty) Ltd, 24 Sturdee Avenue,
Rosebank, Johannesburg 2196, South Africa

Registered Offices: Penguin Books Ltd, 80 Strand, London WC2R 0RL, England

Published by Speak, an imprint of Penguin Group (USA) Inc., 2010

3 5 7 9 10 8 6 4 2

Copyright © Jonathan Friesen, 2010
All rights reserved

LIBRARY OF CONGRESS CATALOGING-IN-PUBLICATION DATA
Friesen, Jonathan.
Rush / by Jonathan Friesen.
p. cm.
Summary: A pariah in his town and home for the results of his risk-taking behavior,
eighteen-year-old Jake seeks adrenaline rushes to clear his dark thoughts, but when Salome,
the girl he loves, gets caught up in taking chances, too, the consequences are devastating.
ISBN 978-0-14-241258-9 (pbk.)
[1. Risk-taking (Psychology)—Fiction. 2. Interpersonal relations—Fiction.
3. Emotional problems—Fiction. 4. Wildfires—Fiction. 5. Firefighters—Fiction.
6. Family life—California—Fiction. 7. California—Fiction.] I. Title.
PZ7.F91661Rus 2010
[Fic]—dc22   2009049934

Speak ISBN 978-0-14-241258-9

Printed in the United States of America

INTO THE FLAMES

Ten minutes later we get our orders, and we jog, geared up, onto the tarmac. We swing into the helicopter beneath the thumping of rotors. In the distance, a finger of black spirals into the sky.

This moment answers all the questions. The "why" Salome doesn't understand and the reason I'll never comply with Dad's request. Inside, I burn a joyful burn, and darkness flees. I hate fire. I want to kill it. But I love it. It dances in my mind.

We hover over the smoke. Radio scratches in the distance.

"Abort, guys. Wind shifts in the canyon." The copter pilot looks back and smiles. "It's turning ugly. Not your war today."

Nobody pays attention. We stare at Moxie's shadow. A red light flashes across his face.

"Hover!" Mox steps out onto the helicopter's skids. "The IC has the call, and this IC says, yeehaw!" Mox tucks into the pike position, pats his belly bag, and disappears down his rappelling rope.

"Guess it is our war," I say to Harv. "Later."

Finding our safety zone. Securing the eighty-pound K-bag filled with saws and food, axes and survival equipment. There will be time for all that. But not now. I stand on the skid and stare out over the sea of green. Smoke rises from beneath the canopy of trees and sends spindly fingers up to grab me. It's down there, waiting to destroy or be destroyed.

I zip down the line into the suffocating cloud. My feet hit Koss's hands, and I hear curses and laughter. I slow. We descend together. The thicker the smoke, the clearer I think. The cloud that fogs my mind blows away, and I'm all here. Right now. Let there be light.

OTHER BOOKS YOU MAY ENJOY

ACKNOWLEDGMENTS

I want to thank an incredible family—mine. Wendy, you know just what to say, and Emma, Isaac, and Si, you know just when to show up with hugs. I love you all.

I also want to mention the incredible people who worked behind the scenes, yet whose names, if you ask me, belong on the book cover. Deidre, agent extraordinaire, I begin with you, and the family that is the Knight Agency. What a team you make. Angelle, you need to know that as an editor, you're a writer's dream. Along with all the good folk at Penguin, your insight makes writing a joy.

I'd be remiss if I didn't mention Cec Murphey. You were there when this idea was merely a crumb, but you believed in the story, and you believed in me. Thank you.

Mom and Dad, you were there too. You support me in more ways than I can list. I'm blessed.

One of the greatest surprises during this season of life has been all the wonderful people at Hillman. You surrounded our family with more love than we could have imagined.

Which brings me to God. Simply acknowledging you feels too small. You're awesome.

Finally, Eli, I humbly thank you for living the life, for leaping into flames when the rest of us flee. You and those who fight fire everywhere are heroes.

FORMER MEMBERS OF THE RUSH CLUB

Christian Kodrey
1987–2010

Allen Kimm
1988–2009

Ray Torea
1988–2009

Carter Ramirez
1985–2008

David Hendersly
1985–2006

Benjamin Graft
1984–2004

Andrew Lee
1981–2002

Jason Graft
1980–2001

Gabe Filcher
1977–2001

CHAPTER 1

"PURE INSANITY."

I whisper at the sky as sheets of rain sting my face. Water rushes by me, swamps my boots, and fills Carver's Gorge up to my shins. It's a steamy wet, a loud wet. Sheer walls rise on both sides and jumble the sounds of foam and thunder. Miles away at Brockton High, teachers drone on about the composition of rocks and good poetry. But in this deep ravine sliced into forests of California pine, my world is wild and alive.

Lightning sears into the rushing flow twenty paces beyond me. I feel the jolt, and my sopped hair leaps.

"Did you feel that?" Troy's hand squeezes my shoulder.

"I'm serious, Jake. If Cheyenne finds me dead, she'll kill me."

I stretch my neck, work my shoulders, and feel my smile widen. "No, she won't. Why do you think she dropped out when you did? She married you for your money and that big old firefighters' insurance policy." I grab his arm and pull him beside me. "She asked me to take you down here so she could collect."

"Shut up! When you and Salome finish playing around and get serious, you'll know what I'm talking about."

I run my hand hard over my forehead. "She's a friend."

I swipe beads of water off my watch with my thumb and peer through the smeary face: 1:30 P.M.

"You wanted to stay in shape in the off-season. I thought a fire boy like you would love all this water." Suddenly, the stone beneath me shifts, and I reach for Troy to steady myself. He whacks at my hand, and I slip to my knees, stand with a laugh.

"Okay, buddy. We're going the length of the gorge in fifty minutes." I point at a boulder that juts out of the froth. "And you, no mercy."

Troy squints and whips back matted hair. "I can't see a thing down here. I'm heading out."

"Follow!" I slap his shoulder and sigh, knowing he

won't go back without me. "Good to have you home."

I leap into darkness. Deep in the cut of the forest, stone and shadow keep it dusk, but beneath this storm, it's midnight. I dodge left, weave right. I wade blind. Massive rocks loom colorless—only lightning gives me a flicker of sight.

"Slow down, Jake! Can't hardly see you."

"It's gonna be close," I call over my shoulder, and my arm grazes a boulder. "Keep up."

I don't fear the granite giants—hit, bleed, run on— it's the ankle twisters, the sunken stone grenades that wait to explode my feet and drop me to my knees.

Rain thickens. Straight-down rain that reaches from the sky deep into the earth.

More lightning sizzles into the canyon walls. The river's on sulfury fire, each breaker tinged blue or gold.

I'm inside a fireworks display, part of the explosion.

Lightning flashes again, and I burn, a pulsing burn that scampers up my legs and sets my spine on fire. The flash steals my strength and leaves me twitching.

I'm not breathing.

I stop, suck air hard, and expand tingling lungs. Troy crashes into me, and my body slumps against a trunk, thin and rough. I gasp and press my cheek against the bark. It feels alive, like I'm alive. Pines that dot the ravine's bottom prove it—there's life down here. I will not die here, not today.

"What happened there?" Troy's voice sounds tinny, but he's yelling in my ear.

"Light—lightning."

I straighten, clench my teeth, and stumble forward. But I can't stand against the flow.

I scrape against rock, leave a hunk of fleshy thigh. My foot slips. My ankle rolls beneath my weight, and I scream. I splash into foaming water face-first.

Troy's strong arms circle my waist and haul me vertical. "Jake, what's the quickest way out? I didn't survive all those fires to get killed in the water!"

"Off me! I need to beat my record."

I pull free from Troy and pause. Something thick and weighty wraps my calves, and I kick it away. A battered jacket dips beneath the surface, swirls, and snags on a rock. I lean over and pick up the shred. Brown leather, with an *I* emblazoned in gold across the back. Caked blood splotches cover the sleeves, the front. My heartbeat races, lit up by a different jolt.

"The Immortals," I whisper, laying the jacket gently on an outcrop.

According to legend, each year at least one member of the underground firefighters' brotherhood must die.

But all that's known is rumor, because dead firemen never speak, and the living strut around Brockton in their Immortals jackets just as tight-lipped.

Whoever they are, they live life short and wild. Like I do.

I stroke the jacket. "Remember how we used to pretend? We'd stick that yellow tape on all our coats?"

Troy nods. "That was before Salome's brother . . . What are you going to do with it?"

I say nothing.

"They're cursed. Cheyenne says if you put one on, the Reaper's at your door." He slaps my shoulder. "You know she's right. I mean, I still see Drew hanging there. I have nightmares about that day."

My heartbeat skips, slows. Death was here. Not the gentle guy who comes for grandpas while they sleep. The violent one, the too-soon one—the one who has a summer home in Brockton.

"It could have been Ray's," I say. "Didn't they find him upstream?"

I close my eyes and see Ray's smile and hear his laugh. I stretch out my other hand and lay it on all that remains of the young firefighter.

Troy nods. "Or Allen. Did he ever show up?"

I shake my head.

"And no others went while I was gone?"

"Just Christian, but they found his body miles from here."

I lift up the jacket and push one arm through.

Troy grabs my free forearm. "Don't!"

I wiggle into leather, cool against warm skin. "You know the difference between them and me? I don't need the jacket. I'm already immortal."

Voices.

Troy glances at me. I give my head a quick shake. "There's nobody else down here."

I strain to see ahead. Lightning flashes and thunder quakes the canyon.

I test my twisted ankle, wince, and peek at my leg. Rain traces pink down my calf, pools and swirls and washes away.

"Let's go," I say.

I slosh forward. That leather scrap steals my will. The creature inside me that needs adrenaline to survive shuts up—it's time to go home.

"Dustin!" a voice shouts out from around the bend.

"Someone's really stupid," I say to Troy. There'll be twenty feet of water before the voice knows it. Troy takes off toward the sound. I grimace and slosh forward and freeze.

Ten people huddle together. Turned out from the circle, a ranger bangs his walkie-talkie on his thigh, curses as water drops off the brim of his cap. Troy's gray-on-black silhouette approaches him. All this I see; I hear nothing. Eerie. The storm allows no noise but its own roar. We step nearer until I hear the ranger's words, see the desperation he hides beneath that brim.

Women cry, and a little kid shrieks from her seat on a granite slab. Men shine flashlights into the sky and holler. I follow the useless beams, look back at the girl.

"Jake!" Troy spins me around. "He says there's a boy stuck—"

"You're a firefighter. Can you get her, and all of them, out of here?"

Troy nods.

I hobble into the circle. "What are you all doing? In less than an hour, water will be above that girl's head."

A man, drippy-faced and hoarse, grabs me. "My son. He's on that cliff—"

I squint upward. *There's no way a kid could climb—*

"Daddy!"

I shield my eyes from the pounding rain, but the small voice is invisible. All above is shadow.

"Hang on, son." Dad sloshes to the rock wall, reaches

for a hold. His fingers slip. "Don't let go!" He runs his hands through soaked hair and stares around with wild eyes.

The little girl whimpers and rocks. I wade toward her perch. "Is that your brother up there?"

She nods.

"I'm Jake King. What's your name?"

"Nikki."

I bend over. "Look at me." She balls up, squeezes her knees to her chin, and peeks.

"I'm gonna bring your brother down. I prom— I guarantee it."

Her small voice whispers, "I shouldn't have called Dusty a dummy."

Troy grabs the shoulders of two rangers. "Hey! You have no time. Get the girl and the family and get out, now!" He turns to me. "You need anyone?"

"Dad," I say.

Troy nods. "The father stays here!"

One ranger grabs the other's sleeve. "It's what I've been telling you. We need to get them out, or we lose 'em."

I look to Troy. "Take them back the way we came." I pick at the zipper on the jacket. "Please don't tell Salome about this."

"What are you gonna do? Your ankle. Your leg—"

"We're leaving." The drippy ranger gestures with his walkie-talkie. "Now!"

Anguish sloshes around me. A mother, heels dug in, fights off men, and Nikki wails.

"Why'd your friend take them away?" Dad speaks to me without emotion.

I walk by his question, stroke the sandpaper rock face. "Wait for Dusty here. And be sure to remind Nikki it wasn't her fault."

I bear full weight on my bad leg, grit my teeth, and climb. Pruned fingertips search for crevices, boots plunge into nooks, and I press hard against the rock.

"Keep screaming, kid!"

"Daddy." It's fainter.

Ten feet, twenty. I reach thirty feet, find a hold, and breathe hard. "More—keep talking! Can't see you."

"Is Daddy coming up?"

To the left.

I veer horizontal across the cliff and continue my climb. Forty feet. I peek down into the darkness. I've reached the Coffin Zone.

I scan the rock face—still can't see him. I close my eyes. The jacket I wear weighs heavy on my arms. Right now I'm one of the Immortals. I'm doing everything they do. Except die.

"Kid! Keep talking!"

"I didn't mean to do it."

Rain pelts my eyes, and I push up. My hand slides onto a flat space, grazes a small pine and the small shoe of a small kid latched onto a tree. I scramble up and lean back against rock. My ankle screams, and my heartbeat slows.

The ledge is four feet wide, two feet deep, with a tree. Far as I remember, this is the only ledge on this rock face. This kid's life is charmed.

Dusty is in second grade, I bet. He doesn't look hurt; his jeans and Celtics T-shirt are nothing but wet. But his makeshift belt makes me smile—a long coil of climbing rope that snakes around his feet.

"Hey there." I pat his back, and he tenses. "I'm Jake. Are you Dusty?"

He doesn't speak.

"I ask because Dusty's dad is down there waiting for him, and if you're not him, I need to keep looking."

"I'm him!" He whips his head around, but he's not letting go of the tree.

"Do you like storms?" I ask. "You get quite a view from up—"

"I hate thunder!" Dusty cries. "It's too loud!"

"It sure is." I lay my hand on his shoulder, feel the

tremble. "There's someone waiting for me, too. And when I don't show up at her place, she's gonna smack me. Hard. Look here." I slip off the jacket and roll up my T-shirt sleeve. "This bruise? That's what happened when I told her I was skipping school today."

Dusty stretches his neck, gets a close look. "That's big. You let a girl do that to you?"

I grin. "More times than you know."

Dusty's teeth chatter, and he turns back toward his tree. "You shouldn't skip school. Didn't your dad write you a note?"

My throat burns. "Nope."

"My dad wrote *me* a note," he says. "He'd probably write you one if you asked him."

"Sounds like you have a great dad." My burn is a dull ache, and I rub my neck. "Here's the only thing. I can get you down, but you have to leave your tree. You need to let go of it and hold on to me."

Dusty shakes his head. "I didn't mean to get lost. Nikki kept calling me that name. I thought our rope would go to the bottom." He stares at me with his serious face. "She called me a dummy."

I turn my head and suck in a laugh.

"I tied it to a tree on top and climbed down. But I'm not too good at knots and I fell—"

"You are the bravest, luckiest fifteen-year-old—"

"I'm only eight!"

I tousle his hair. "Eight-year-old."

I look over the rope: fifty feet and sound. "I'm wrapping this around you, around me, even this tree. Keep hugging it." I thread and knot and weave a harness for Dusty. "Okay, big man. You're going to hate me for two minutes, but I guarantee, then you'll like me."

"I like you." He turns, and I yank his body toward me. He screams.

"Dusty!" Dad hollers up.

I stand, brace against the tree, and lower Dusty. He shrieks the entire way down.

Fifty feet below, screaming stops and crying starts.

"Thank you!" Dusty's dad hollers it again and again. I've never heard a man so grateful, but he's not leaving. Fool.

"How can I thank you?"

"You can get out of this gorge!" I shout down at them.

They head out the direction we came in, and I curl up to watch the storm. Thunder rumbles the ledge, and I feel it deep inside my chest. His dad wrote him a note. Nice dad.

CHAPTER 2

IT'S SIH BEFORE I scooter back into Brockton. Nestled in California's San Llamos Valley, the town shows no sign of the storm. No pooling in the ditch fronting Brass Rail Tack, no mud on the Bulldogs baseball diamond. The town is the same now as it was this morning—dry and tough, without much sign of life.

I accelerate, turn left onto Celia Street, and start past the paper mill. It takes a block to finish the job. Hanking's Mill is its own sprawling city, complete with on-site doctor, cafeteria, and sleepers for when workers need to double back or escape their homes for a night. Divided into eight separate buildings for fire-protection purposes, the mill anchors Brockton on the map and, as Dad owns it, secures most residents in his back pocket.

Hank King has seen to everything, just as Grandpa did before him. And he's earned Brockton's respect. Or maybe owns it.

It's shift change, and millers float out like clouds, break up when they get to the street. I slow and weave between them, pop out near the loop that snakes up One Rock Hill. I back-and-forth on the scooter, reach two brick homes with killer views. I pause and watch a helicopter fly low overhead. Its rhythmic thump softens into the distance. It flies toward the gorge—probably out looking for Dusty's mysterious rescuer.

Dad kneels in front of our Tudor and coils the garden hose. The manicured lawn, the Roman fountain, the vines climbing the trellis; there's nothing out of place.

"Dad!" I topple my wheels, wince, and hobble up the drive. "You won't believe this."

He doesn't turn. Dad sets the hose aside and strokes the wildflowers in Mom's wildflower garden. Today, like every day, he spends hours caring for that garden—the last thing Mom created before she packed up her pottery wheel and anxiety disorder and left. I approach quiet and slow. "Hey, Dad—"

"Bell 205 or Bell 212?"

"I didn't pay attention. It was just a helicopter. Listen—"

"'Just a helicopter.' Do you know how many times they saved my life?" Dad rises, looks me head to toe. "School called."

"I know, but if you could've seen—"

He raises his hand. A huge hand, like mine.

Dad inhales long and loud. "There's nothing you could say right now to help your situation, so cut the excuses."

I wish him dead. Right here on the front lawn. Then I wish him resurrected because I need him.

"You should let me finish." I step toward him, peek down at the garden.

Scottie pushes out the front door, bounds down the steps.

"That was a 212, right? What's going on?"

Dad muscles his arm around him: my fresh-from-the-shower, perfect older brother. I look at myself, at the blood and grime and swollen ankle.

"Be proud of your brother. Mark the day. On January the twenty-first, Scottie King followed in the footsteps of every true Brockton man." Dad tears up—an occurrence I've not seen in years—and my stomach turns. "He was picked up by Brockton Hand Crew Number

One. After his two years in Montana, they took him on reputation alone."

I stare at my brother and force a smile. "So you're back for good?"

He sets his jaw, steps out from Dad's grip. "Not just me. Kyle's back. Picked up by Mox's rappel crew. You probably already heard from Troy. Rumor has it he and Cheyenne will be based here, too."

"Yeah, I just saw him, which brings me to what I was—"

"Quite a homecoming." Dad steps forward and reattaches his hand to my brother's shoulder. "Quite a gain for Brockton and the Forest Service."

I'm going to puke. The wildfire crews that spread out over California during fire season base in our town. My grandpa's grandpa fought fires in summer and lined his pockets at the mill. It's what we do. Who we are.

Well, who *they* are. With the triumphant return of Scottie and his crowd from their first two years of fighting, Dad will strut twenty-four/seven.

I glance at Scottie and nod. "That's good. That's great. Wildfires won't stand a chance." I look back to Dad, slowly point at our house. "But if you walk in that door and quick flip on the news, I bet you'll see—"

"I don't want my evening ruined by whatever stunt

you pulled. Not tonight. I'm taking this man out to celebrate. It's been three years since I turned full attention to the mill and lay down my Brockton ax. It's about time the next King picked it up." He pats Scottie and steps toward me. "Maybe by watching Scottie's choices, some wisdom will rub off on you." Dad walks toward his truck and gets in. The door slams.

Scottie and I stare at each other. Today was inevitable. The feds and his homecoming were inevitable. But he could've waited until tomorrow. I try to speak, but kind words stick.

"He shouldn't be so hard," Scottie says. "He was talking like you were coming to dinner, too, until the high school called. What happened today?"

I shake my head. "Nothing."

"Nothing," he says, and tongues the inside of his cheek. "It doesn't have to always go down like this. Lose the death wish." Scottie gives my shoulder a gentle shove, glances down at my bloody legs. "Some of us would like to keep you arou—"

His mouth hangs open, but his gaze is locked, fixed on what dangles from my hand. He leans over and lifts the limp, leathery arm of the Immortals jacket.

"Yours?"

"Course not. Found it in Carver's Gorge." I extend

it for Scottie to inspect. "You see any of these in Montana?"

"Yeah. There was one walking around." He shakes his head. "The guy wearing it wasn't the type to answer questions." Scottie lets go of the leather. "Does Salome know you have—"

"No, and she won't, right?"

Scottie exhales loud. "You're messing with a curse, brother. It starts with those jackets and fills this whole town." He takes a step toward the truck.

I force a smile. "Yeah, Troy told me. But you came back anyway."

"I did. Have my reasons." Scottie turns, pauses, and looks over his shoulder. "You might want to lose that."

CHAPTER 3

I'M NOT ON THE EVENING NEWS.

There's a joyful dad, a shaken boy, and a still-sobbing girl. They call me Spider-Man. They call me the Good Samaritan.

Good Samaritan. I pace the garage. *Salome will like that.*

I can't be in this house when the two Musketeers return. I turn the brown jacket over in my hands, then plop down onto concrete. I bury my head in my arms and slow my breathing. Dark clouds roll into my mind, and their shadows eclipse clear thoughts. One way out: that's all I have. Only a rush of adrenaline clears the head, and I won't find that while crumpled on a slab of cement.

I squeeze back into the jacket, scooter across town through the black night, and park in the shadow of Brockton High.

I'm in search of climbing rope and know where to find it. I race around to the back of the gym and scan the entrance. The athletic door stands thick and gray and windowless. It opens freely, and I slip inside.

The sounds of bouncing basketballs and teachers' voices echo through the halls. Their Friday-night pickup game is a heated affair. I scamper past the open gym door and duck into the boys' locker room. There I weave around benches to the equipment storage.

"Bingo." The thin climbing rope coils in the corner. I'll bring it back on Monday.

I grab it, hoist it over my shoulder, and slip out of the school. Minutes later, I hide my scooter in tall grass beneath the old water tower. And climb.

The evil clamp around my brain loosens a turn, and I increase my speed. If little Maddie from my YMCA climbing class were here, I'd slow down and lecture her on the importance of good footholds. But tonight my only friend is the invisible one who never leaves.

Depression. Panic attacks. Suicidal tendencies. Professionals have given my head many labels. But they've never *heard* me. This darkness in my head, it's a separation from the world. A confusion thick as soup.

It's a brain cloud.

"Hey, Monkey Boy. How high are ya going?"

Salome?

I peek around the tube of concrete on which I hang and stare down at Winders Street, lit and quiet on a Friday night. The street is dead, except for a plastic bag that flutters like a drunken butterfly along the tar. It dodges and weaves and stops—pressed beneath the foot of a beautiful girl. A beautiful girl who isn't Salome. She bends down and picks it up, carries it toward the tower, and stares up. My stomach drops.

"This yours?" she asks. "Hey! Did you join the Immor—"

"Go on home, Brooke."

"Ellie's mom is in San Diego for the weekend." She talks so loud, Ellie's mom is liable to hear her. "Why don't you stop in after you're finished doing . . . whatever you're doing?"

"Yeah. Maybe."

She flips her hair, folds her arms, and watches me. Like she's witnessing the postman out delivering mail. Like it's downright common to see a guy hanging from an old water tower in the middle of the night.

My arms swing from one twisted shaft of metal to another. Higher, always higher. Rough hands grasp rusted gray rungs, the remnant of a ladder not climbed in years. Callused feet strain for a toehold, and I push toward the peak, toward the word BROCKTON.

Wind whistles and hints at another storm, but each upward swing whooshes away more of the cloud that muddies my mind. With each reach, the distance between me and Brockton stretches like taffy. The town's grip weakens, its tentacles bust. Give me food, and I'll stay up here forever.

"Jake!" Brooke's sharp laugh cuts through the breeze.

I climb higher, reach for the final rung, and wish this tower were sixty feet taller. My hand brushes twigs. I pull up, my face level with a bird's nest. Five little mouths strain at me.

Mom bird screeches, flies toward me. I duck and bash my forehead against metal. The angry crow flies at the back of my neck.

I scamper to the top and stare out into blackness, waiting for my heart to pound. But it thumps on, slow and steady and dead.

Laughter, faint and harsh. From the villa, temporary housing for firefighter crews that blow in for the fire season. The villa stands vacant now, except for the year-round crazies who sleep during the day and come out at night. They say the Immortals are like vampires. Only wilder.

Their husky voices vanish and Brooke's figure disappears and silence thickens.

I start to uncoil the rope, and pause. My brain feels like it's shrinking. I toss the rope to the side.

I stand and close my eyes and lean back out over the railing. No relief. I drop down and sit and dangle my feet. My brain still feels black. I grip the rail, slide legs forward off the catwalk, and let my body hang. I look down sixty feet below, at the headlamps of a toy car. It creeps directly below me and falls dark.

The distance from me to it, it's beautiful.

Night gusts blow strong. I close my eyes and release one hand. High above the town, my heart flutters, and I smile. Forearm muscles fire and relax. My brain cloud breaks. I stare up at my grip, slowly slide my pinky off the rail.

A jolt deep in my gut kick-starts my heart. I let my ring finger slip free.

I dangle from two fingers and a thumb, and the day feels right.

My hand shakes, tenses. Wind, chill—I feel it all.

Pain shoots through my palm, and my pointer finger twitches rhythmically.

The railing cracks.

My sight sharpens, locks on the next section of catwalk. I need to latch on to keep from falling, but my thoughts clear. In this moment, I'm falling and alive.

I'm Jake King, small and stupid and reeling with a glorious panic.

My free hand shoots up toward solid pipe, and I slide my cramped claw onto the secure section.

Metal snaps, and the busted section falls away.

I watch the chunk of metal fall silently through the night, and my stomach sinks with it. I know where it will land; I see the toy car.

It smashes the windshield, and all is quiet. A horrible quiet. There is no scream, no horn that blares. Just a twisted metal rail stabbed into the top of a car.

I pull myself to the catwalk and peek over the edge. There's a twinge in my gut, then a slow burn. It finds dry tinder and ignites. I should climb down. The Good Samaritan should help, but I can't. I double over and squeeze my chest.

From below, a noise.

A car door creaks open, and a leg fights its way out.

"Oh," I whisper. "Oh, no."

CHAPTER 4

"THE SCHOOL BOARD VOTES to expel Jake
King for the remainder of the year and to deny his can-
didacy to graduate in the spring."

I turn to Dad and whisper, "I didn't even *use* their
rope."

There are murmurs behind me, satisfied whispers.
I glance over my shoulder. Faces smirk and heads nod.
If Dad turned around, those happy lips would squeeze
tight, but he doesn't.

"Finally, justice falls on this criminal!" Mr. Ramirez
rises, double-fists the table to my left, strides around
toward us. He leans over me, hands balled tight. His

gaze shifts from Dad to me and back again.

"Control your son, Hank," he whispers. "Or someone else will." Mr. Ramirez slaps the table, and I jump.

"I'm so sor—"

He vanishes out the door.

Dad doesn't even twitch. He sits and stares at the Council of Eight who just ruined my life.

Three of them wriggle beneath that stare, reach for water glasses. Their lives at Hanking's Mill just became much more uncomfortable.

But not Superintendent Haynes. He's in his glory. The pockmark-faced geezer stares at me.

"Next order of business—"

Dad leans into my shoulder. "Come on, son."

I stand, and we walk out side by side.

One step outside the administration building and I know my life has changed. People who came to support the Ramirezes turn their backs, pretend to mill about. Angry people who'll never know about Dusty. They whisper and mutter, then whisper again. "Jake had it coming. It's about time."

I know Kyle Ramirez is busted up bad—face, ribs, arms. It's my fault that he's sliced and scarred. But I only wanted to lose the confusion for a little while.

My gaze flits and searches and locks onto the Lees, silent and still. Salome's parents push forward. Jacob pats Dad's back, and Mrs. Lee hugs me tight.

"I love you, Jake," she whispers. "Salome's waiting up." She straightens, breathes deep. "She couldn't bear to see it. Come over tonight."

Our neighbors spin and walk away. I fix my gaze on them, and the crowd goes mute. I want them back.

Dad stares at his employees, daring them to speak. His arm rounds my shoulder. "We walk together."

It's been years since I felt this hand, and then only to welt my rear. I glance at him, at his proud face. My punishment is about him; it has to be. He takes this personally. Otherwise, that hand would be at home, flipping channels from the couch.

Officer Rogers steps up. "You could've been charged. You got off easy."

"Nobody gets off easy," Dad says. "You know this wasn't deliberate. Do your job, Max."

Max disperses those gathered, and Dad pulls me through what's left of the self-righteous pack, down the walkway that leads to our car. Dad's steps slow. I know he's tired, that I make him that way.

I swallow hard. "Dad, I—"

He grabs me by the jacket and jams me hard against the Suburban. Muscles in his face tense, and his teeth grind.

"You screwed up." He presses harder, then releases. Presses again, and lets go. I let him try to squeeze the bad out of me, the hungry monster he doesn't understand and Mom never understood and I can't explain.

Dad stares into me. "Do you have any idea how much I love you?"

I mouth no and shake my head. He yanks me close and whispers. "Why, Jake?"

The two of us stand and hug, surrounded by all the anger Brockton can muster.

SALOME LEE PACES IN OUR driveway, squints as our headlamps cross her face. She bites her lip, folds and unfolds her arms. She walks up to the Suburban and, like a trick candle Brockton can't blow out, brightens my dark night. I step out, and she hugs me.

I put my arms around her and let my face fall into her hair. I breathe deep and inhale a scent I smell nowhere else in this town. I'm not worth this moment, because Salome won't hug another guy—least I haven't seen it happen in eighteen years. Every young man within one hundred miles has tried to worm his way to where I am, but she's too smart. Salome knows what they want. Besides, she says they're a waste of her time. She says she already knows.

I know what she means. Though I act dumb, I know exactly what she means and what she wants. I want it, too. But I can't. Not tonight, not ever. Because everyone who touches my craziness gets hurt; just ask Kyle. And I won't let her hurt. I'd die first.

"Salome, they booted me," I whisper.

The squeeze tightens. "How far?"

"The super has a big foot."

"For the entire year? They won't let you graduate?" She steps back, away from me, and forces a smile. "*The Brockton High Gazette* asked me to cover the hearing. I only got as far as the angle: 'Why Do Accidents Equal Expulsions?'"

"They'll change your headline. Something about stolen school property used in Jake's latest screwup."

Salome frowns. "So their decision's final? I mean, maybe if you confess to all the physics answers you stole from me, they'll let you out on parole." She runs out of air and closes her eyes. Salome rubs her arms on a suddenly chilly evening.

Dad's car door slams. "Say your good-byes, Salome. Jake? Inside."

I grab her elbow and lean closer. "You've cheated off me, too."

"When?" Her hands shoot to her hips.

"Preschool. I peed in that little potty, and who took the credit? Huh? What do you say to that?"

Salome balls up her hand and swings. Her knuckle finds the sweet spot on my shoulder and deadens my arm. "You're sick."

"Yeah." I run my hand through dark hair. "Maybe I am."

Salome starts the slow walk to the house next door. She pauses halfway, turns. "I wanted to come tonight. But I can't see them hate you like they do." She steps nearer, raises her arms, and lets them flop at her sides. "Why can't anyone see past the outside? No one knows you. How can you stand it?"

I lock fingers behind my neck and stare at the sky. "You know me." I lower my gaze. "That's one."

Salome nods. "You have one. You'll always have one." She vanishes into her home.

Crickets fill the silence with irritating chirps, and I raise my gaze to Scottie's window. My big brother stands in the dim light with his arms crossed. I smile weakly and raise my hand. He rubs his face. His blinds drop.

I stare at my house and fight backward through a

foggy mind . . . to last Friday. There. I glance at the bottom step, where I stood when Dad pushed past me with Scottie. That's when I had the idea. By the top step I had planned the climb. I did it right. I did everything right, but . . . I gaze into the family room, where Dad sat quietly that night while I told him I likely killed Scottie's best friend.

It's been three days. Kyle has to hear "I'm sorry" from me.

I run inside and grab the keys. Dad's already in the shower, scrubbing and muttering and cursing.

I burst back out onto the drive. Salome waits on her steps. Writing, always writing in that journal. She reads my mind, again, and knows where I'm headed.

"I'm coming with you."

WE STEP INTO BROCHTON MEDICAL. Still and spotless, with the stench of sick people. Filled with old folks, the barely staffed "hospital" is more a glorified nursing home. Not many here are under seventy, nurses included.

Salome leans into my shoulder, pats my chest. "Kyle might not want to see you."

"I'm not thrilled to see myself."

"Come on." She grabs my arm and yanks me down

the hall. Ms. Roberts stacks up her Sudoku books. Another busy day at the information desk.

"I'd like to see Kyle," I say.

She stares up from behind her spectacles, her face emotionless. "Why?"

I'm not ready for that, and for once my mouth stays shut.

Salome kicks me in the calf and shoves me to the side. "We're here to see how he's doing."

I reach down and rub my leg. I scowl and glance at my attacker. She looks great from any angle. Really great. One hundred percent pure compassion. She tosses back blond hair and blinks those extra-strength blues. If she'd have crushed Kyle, they'd probably have given her a medal.

"I'm sure any young man would enjoy seeing *you*, Salome."

My calf throbs, and I massage again, mutter, "From a safe distance—"

Salome's hand smacks my face and covers my mouth. Hidden by the desk, Ms. Roberts can't see her brutal side; nobody else can.

I'm no longer in this conversation. I roll my eyes, stand, and step back. *When you two work this all out, call me. I'll be in the waiting room.*

I turn and haul toward the chairs. More words of compassion behind me. Salome's working hard; she always does.

"Get back here, Jake," Salome calls. "We have five minutes."

I hustle back to the counter. "Thanks, Ms. Roberts."

Her eyes stay fixed on my best friend.

Salome sighs, reaches over the counter, and squeezes Ms. Roberts's hand. "Thank you."

The fossil breaks into a smile. "You're so welcome, dear."

"Crap," I mutter, and follow Salome to the elevators. "You could kill someone and—"

"No, I couldn't. Now shut up." Her finger toys with the Up button, then pulls back. "His dad's here."

I nod. "Press it."

We reach the third floor; the doors open. Mr. Ramirez stands legs apart and arms folded. His face is blaze red. He sees Salome, looks down, and curses. Once again, I disappear.

"Why are you here, Salome?" Mr. Ramirez asks.

"My friend is here to visit your son." She looks at me and smiles. "I'm here with my friend."

"Visit my son . . ." Mr. Ramirez says, and elevator doors begin to shut. He and I both stick out our arms.

They touch. He recoils, and Salome and I step out of the elevator.

"Why did you do this to my Kyle?"

I close my eyes and watch the railing fall. It smashes the car, and my eyelids jolt open. He won't believe me. He'll think I was up there with a hacksaw waiting for Kyle to drive beneath me. But I wasn't. I didn't yell bull's-eye. I wanted to throw up.

"None of it was on purpose. I want to tell him how sorry—"

"You'll tell him nothing until you tell me the truth."

I glance at Salome. She looks down. I know she's praying.

"All I know is why I climbed. Well, I sort of know." I massage my forehead, then look at him square. "I climbed the old water tower because it's the tallest thing in Brockton, because all the way up the ladder is busted, and anytime I could fall."

Salome shifts. I know she can't stand hearing what I do. I peek at her. She fidgets with her heart-shaped locket.

"I'm sorry," I whisper.

She shakes her head, and I turn back to Mr. Ramirez.

"I reached the top because I'm strong and I never

fall. I climbed around the tower on the old catwalk. I found the soundest section of railing and hung." I scuff the white hospital floor, wipe off the smudge with my boot. "But the metal wasn't strong enough. I didn't know who was beneath me. I didn't think the rail could break." I breathe deep and look him in the eye, whisper, "I didn't know."

I clear my throat. "I like Kyle. I mean, he's Scottie's best friend. I'm sorry."

Mr. Ramirez balls his hands. "You're a crazed menace, Jake King." He lowers his voice. "Leave."

He doesn't know how it feels when blood explodes from your heart, whips through your body, and, for a second, everything is clear and real. He doesn't understand why I climb or jump, why I can't stop climbing or jumping.

"Okay." I get back on the elevator. "Tell Kyle I was here. Could you tell him that?"

"Mr. Ramirez, you don't know Jake." Salome shakes her head. "I know you think you do, but—"

"Stay, Salome." Mr. Ramirez lowers his voice, and I stick out my foot to hold the elevator door.

"Kyle's weak. Cut up real bad," he says. "He lost blood, and there'll be many scars. He protected Allison with his own body. Must be that firefighter's instinct."

He straightens. "It's a good thing he'll have time to heal before fire season. But you must know that he used to speak of you often. Seeing you would cheer him up."

Salome looks into the elevator, frowns, and mouths, He was *protecting* Allison?

Out loud she says, "Wait for me in the lobby." She gently pushes my toe with hers. "Be right down." She smiles and stares at me until the crack in the doors disappears. I bury my head in my hands. The car starts down, and I punch the Stop button, hang between floors. It feels right. Mr. Ramirez doesn't want me up, Ms. Roberts doesn't want me down. And Dad will be furious when I slink back home.

CHAPTER 5

EXPULSIONS SUCK. They're like house arrest, except I get to leave, but when I do it feels like I should be somewhere else. Everything is always wrong.

Normal guys wouldn't have this problem. Study in the morning and work the night shift at the mill. That's what they'd do. They'd take the GED and get on with their life. That's Dad's plan for me, too, which means even if I could do it, I wouldn't.

Instead, I pace the basement like the lion at the San Diego Zoo, stepping over plastic Wonder bread wrapping. I've squeezed and shaped eight slices into mushy, warped animals, but now the loaf is gone.

The cloud that fills my head thickens. *It's only been two days—*

Eight steps, turn.

—and already I can't think.

Eight steps, turn.

Can't escape either—Dad shifts to silent gear, the one he uses when he's had enough of me. Above my head, he and Scottie make up for my lost words with Forest Service talk. Wildfire stories, wildfire strategies— the season is months away, but they can't stop. Safety zones, fire lines, and the disaster at Mann Gulch are all that matters.

I check my watch: 2:30 P.M. I take the steps and bound up two flights into my room.

"Please, Salome," I whisper. "Come home early."

She knows me, knows I'm losing it. Had my punishment been chopping wood at Boys Town, I could have survived. But it's not. I've been sentenced to a private hell of boredom.

I stare out the window and wait for her to walk up the drive. The doorbell rings. I don't move; it's the best part of the day.

Scottie's footsteps race to the door, and I press my ear to the screen.

"Hi, Salome."

"Hi, Scottie."

I drink in the awkward silence, the kind my brother makes me live in. I close my eyes and imagine his shuffling feet, his forced grin.

"How are you?" Salome asks, free and easy.

"I'm good."

I peek down at my friend, watch her exaggerated nod. "Good, good. Is there any chance I could see Jake?"

"Well, yeah, you—yes. I'm pretty sure he's upstairs. Say, I was going to ask . . ."

Say nothing, Salome . . .

"Forget it." Scottie backs away, and I listen to her marvelous footsteps on the stairs. Sixteen steps. Two knocks.

"Come on in!"

She throws it open, smirks like a cat. "Just once, I want to come over here and have you open that door." She drops her backpack on the floor and herself onto my chair.

Outside, Scottie's truck roars to life, then quiets as he pulls away. "Hearing Scottie fumble is the highlight of my day. That and you showin' up," I look at her, drop my gaze. "I need to lift a cloud, Sal."

She nods and puffs out air. Salome wrings her hands, closes her eyes, and lowers her head to pray.

"Whoa," I say. "We have a deal about the praying thing."

"If you're not keeping your side of it, you have nothing to say to me right now. All I asked is for you to try a short one. You wake up and tell Him hello. That's no more than common courtesy."

"Please, no God-talk now."

"Fair enough." She rolls her lovely eyes and smiles. "No God-talk now. Could you do a movie?" Her voice is soft. "I'll even let you pick out one of those morally bankrupt flicks that cheer you so."

I can't sit through a movie. I can't sit through dinner.

"I'm going jumping at the salvage yard," I say, and point to my head. "Need to. It's pretty dark."

Salome stares at me hard. "Why not wait for your dad to get here? When you disappear, he calls me, and I hate—"

"Can't wait." I grab her arm and raise a finger to my lips. "Shh! Can't you hear it? My dirt bike calls." I release her and grab leather gloves off my desk. "Come with me. One more tweak on that engine and I know I can clear the pile." She wears a thinking face, and I continue, "I'll need someone to verify my jump . . . or pick up the pieces."

Silence. We walk into the garage. Salome stands, arms crossed, and leans against the workbench. She watches me grab tools, search for drivers and wrenches. It's a gentle watch, like she understands, though I know she can't. There's nothing dark in that head, no need to feel deadened nerves fire to life. I stop and stare back. She hums something—I've never heard that from her before.

"Why do you hang around me?" I ask.

"You're good material for the school paper." She picks up sandpaper and smoothes the bench edge. "I could get a Pulitzer writing about your adventures."

"Think you'll ever *not* be around?"

Her blue eyes flash. "No. It's a promise." She glances down. "But things will change in summer. I don't know how much time my journalism classes will take."

I lean against the car and close my eyes.

"Suppose one of us should make something of ourselves." I grab my hair and tug, then force open my fingers.

She walks toward me, lifts my chin, and looks into me. She strokes my head. "It'll pass."

I nod.

"And one day," she continues, "you'll do something

great, something nobody else could do. I know you don't care, but others will notice, and they'll see your courage, and you'll be on the cover of *The New York Times*." Salome's eyes narrow and she looks away, her voice distant. "And maybe I'll write a story about this young man who said no to this town and its fascination with fire and the Immortals and . . . well, I'm just saying I know you'll do something great someday." Salome takes her square of sandpaper and slaps it into my hand.

"I take it you're not coming with me."

She smiles.

Ten minutes later, I have all I need. I load my backpack with Dad's tools and pull my mountain bike from the garage. "If Dad asks where I am, just say—"

"That you're too busy jumping crushed cars to speak with him. Sure thing." Salome tugs at the bedroll tucked beneath my arm and gently grabs my chin. "An overnight?"

I exhale. "If you knew how bad I am right now. It's not as if Dad will care."

She says nothing.

"Fine!" I unstrap the bedroll. "I'll be back before dark."

"Thank you." She sighs and walks toward her house, calls over her shoulder, "I'm not your mom. It was only a question."

I HOP ON MY BIKE and ride out of town. I accelerate past Hanking's Mill and the hundreds of cars parked in the lot. Somewhere in the heart of the building, Dad wanders, staring at his workers. Scottie's with him, I know it. Getting pointers for when the mill will be his, the townspeople will be his.

The road winds around and up into the Sierra Llamos, and two hours later I reach the first peak. Brockton spreads out in the valley beneath like a spider. Here, looking down, I breathe easy, free of the web.

I throw my bike onto the shoulder and hike into the woods. Ten minutes in, trees thin out, and patches of light reach the forest floor. Abruptly the tree line breaks, and I stand, squint, and exhale in brilliant sunshine.

Rusted buses, old bridge trusses, worm-filled railroad ties—the abandoned salvage yard spreads out before me. Acres and acres of castoffs. Treasure gleaming in the sunlight.

I head for the second heap—a giant mountain of metal. Crushed cars, five wide and three tall, form the bulk of the pile. My gaze flits from the takeoff ramp I built to where I'll land. Or wipe out.

I step nearer to a crushed Suburban and touch it. A wave of dark wallops my mind. I peek at the dented lean-to where my dirt bike rests. There's no time to fiddle with the engine. I need a jump now.

I jog toward the bike, pass a rusted water heater, and stop. Height. It's what I need to up the rush. I muscle the tank toward the stack of cars. It's a sweaty job, but I haul the hunk of metal onto a hood, then climb up and pull it higher still.

A throat clears from down below.

"Strangest sculpture I've ever seen. Mom would have liked it."

I rest the heater against a hood and peek down. Scottie stands, arms folded, legs spread—just like Mr. Ramirez had at the hospital.

"So you're talking to me again, huh?" I position the tank and slowly release my hands. It balances.

"Can you blame me for a little silence? Kyle almost died."

I stare back at his controlled face. There's no way to see inside him. He has no tell. Years ago, he used that control at the poker table to take my allowance; now he uses it to piss me off.

I jump down and brush the rust from my gloves onto my jeans. "I know. And I don't know how to apologize any bigger. If I knew a way, I would. Because I hurt everybody, again." I exhale and straighten. "Thing is, he wasn't the only one who almost died that night."

"But you—"

I straighten and stare. "Deserve it?"

Scottie rolls his eyes, and his gaze travels over the crushed cars. The water tank shifts, and I turn, reach up, and balance it.

"Do you need a hand?" he asks.

I nod, and he takes my place. We lug the heater higher in silence, finally roll it onto the top of the pile. I know he can't stay quiet for long.

"What are we doing?" He wipes his forehead with his shirtsleeve.

"I want this tank sticking up on top. I want to jump from there to there." I point at my landing ramp. "And go right over the top of this."

"Impossible."

"Beautiful. There's the difference between us. You wouldn't see beauty if you were leaping over it."

He shakes his head. "And you don't see it when she—it—stands right in front of you."

I frown. There's no tennis match between us. No

spoken volley back and forth. All is serve and smash and game over.

"You didn't come up for the conversation. You didn't come up to help or to watch my leap." I gesture around the dump. "Let's see, that leaves—"

Scottie puffs out air. "I'm here for Dad."

"No surprise there. The man couldn't wait for tonight? Tell me, favored firstborn, what's our father want now?"

"You have extra time now. He wants you to—"

"Work afternoons at the mill. Dad's told me."

Scottie stares, waits, throws up his arms. "You could do something responsible. Wake up, Jake! Do you want everyone thinking you're crazy? Do you like it that everyone hates you?"

I bend an antenna with my foot. "You hate me?"

He starts to speak, but I interrupt.

"And that's not why you're here. Just say—"

"Put your name in with the Forest Service. I bet Dad will make some calls. Some crew will pull your cert, and you'll get picked up." He scowls at the oil on his hands and his polo. "You could be stationed somewhere else and get out of this town. This is me talking, not Dad."

I shake my head. "I didn't think you'd try to sell me the Brockton dream."

"Well, start thinking, because fighting fire could save your butt." Scottie leans over the water heater. "All your wild crap. Those stunts have a place." He exhales. "There's nothing like it when you're out there, heat scorching your—"

I hold up my hand and stare away from my brother. Scottie exhales hard.

"It's great that you found your thing." I catch my breath and lower my voice. "But I need it faster than a hand crew. I need it faster and higher . . . Ever felt a rush like twenty roller coasters blow away every ugly thing inside your head?"

"I don't want to be in your head."

"You think I wake up dreaming of ways to kill myself. I don't. I don't dream at all. I live trying to come up with one clear thought." I jump off the pile and land soft. "You think you offer choices. Those aren't choices. Here's what I got. Find a rush. Push it to the edge. And for a minute, maybe an instant, I'll feel what you feel every moment of every day." I stare at the dirt. "Besides, you know Dad thinks I'm a lunatic. He'd never let a crew see my app."

"I'd put in a word."

I say nothing.

Scottie tightens his lips and nods. "It was an idea, is all." He eases off my pile and kicks a car. "A junk pile. Great place to live a life."

Scottie mutters something about a rip in his shirt and disappears into the woods.

Minutes pass, and the sun's shadow darkens my face.

"Scottie?" I dart after him. "Scottie!" I reach my mountain bike. His truck is gone.

Suddenly, I hate it here. I need to talk to Salome. I strap on my helmet, then bend and check my tires.

I whip the bike around, face toward Brockton. Between us, there's a ten-foot drop off the side of the road and thousands of trees. If I hit it just right, if I weave and cut and hurdle blind like a bat straight down the mountain, I'll be home in twenty minutes. Or I can spend an hour on the road.

"Join the Forest Service," I mutter, and shake my head hard and feel a flutter in my stomach.

I push off the road's shoulder, and for a second I free-fall. The moment is perfect; I'm perfect. Suspended, I have no decisions, feel no pain. In this instant, I can do nothing wrong.

I land hard in brush; my back wheel kicks right, and I carom left, off my normal track.

Faster, faster. I whip by pines, nerves on heavenly fire. I fly down the mountain and start to pedal. Life. It's mine again.

A shadowy trunk reaches out and catches my shoulder. My shirt rips; the bark sandpapers flesh. Tires chatter, lose their line, and I recover at a diagonal. I race too fast to change course. If I pop out of this forest alive, it won't be on the grassy slope gliding into Brockton.

Leg muscles sear. Hair flaps. I hear nothing but the wind tunneling in my ears, and every sense works at maximum. There is this or working at the mill. This deathly life, or a life of death.

"Yah!"

My arm throbs, and I squint back sweat. A hundred microcorrections later, I fly off the mountain's steep top half and rocket across I-10.

Lights flash, and a deep horn blares. A fire truck narrowly misses me and speeds into town. But I'll beat it.

Two more minutes. Trees break, and I veer right. I catch my bearings, pedal perpendicular to the slope, and sweep gently down toward town. My heartbeat slows.

I reach Lydell Street and brake. I imagine the

street in front of me up in flames. I feel the heat, see myself on a crew racing hell-bent to kick the burning monster in the teeth. Inside, a flutter.

Maybe Scottie's not so dumb after all.

CHAPTER 6

TWO WEEKS LATER, OUR doorbell rings. Once, twice. Scottie's not getting it, and I answer.

Kyle.

He's whiter than usual, his face a pasty sheet criss-crossed with scars and dotted with scabs. He stands stiff, like there's a lot of casting holding him together.

"Is Scottie here?" he asks.

"Upstairs. Hey, what I did to you was really—"

Kyle waves his hand and pushes by me. He walks slowly, as if his legs weigh a ton.

"—stupid."

He pauses at the bottom of the stairs. My gaze is

glued to his back, to the gold *I* across the shoulders of his brown leather flight jacket.

"Say, Kyle, is that your jacket? Or is it Carter's old one? Your brother belonged to the Immortals, right? I mean, before his crash—"

Kyle whips around, his face furious. "None of your business, freak. No questions." He slumps into the banister. "In the spin, is all. I'm in the spin."

That jacket plods up our steps. I've seen the jackets walk around town before, but they're different now that I've held one. Usually they swagger. But not the one in the gorge, not Drew's when we found it, and not Kyle's now.

I wait an hour for him to come down. To finish my pathetic apology. To tell him I never meant to hurt him. And to grab him. I want to squeeze his shoulders until he tells me how to join and how to get my brown leather. I need to know what "in the spin" means, because rumor says they're just like me. Crazy. Without fear and without a future in this world.

But Kyle doesn't leave and I'm late for my first day back at the YMCA and I can't wait to see little Maddie. I've missed all the kids from climbing class, especially her, and wonder how high she's climbed.

***

I STROLL THROUGH THE Y'S glass doors and into the lobby. I pause and blink. A wave of black floats across my thoughts. *Not now.* I shake my head hard, but the clouds don't break, and my feet shuffle on autopilot. They carry me into the empty gym.

I slap blue mats onto the floor beneath the climbing wall and rub my hands across the rough rock face. It's fake, just like Ms. Jameson's enthusiasm when she agreed to let me teach again, but that's fine. I'm here, and soon Mads will be, too.

My feet test the wall, and I throw myself against it, scamper to the top. I climb up and across, hang and flop onto my back. I am Spider-Man, and when my feet hit the mats and I check the time, I wish I had a mask.

Not one of seven kids shows up. Not even Mads.

I plunk onto the blue, make a mat angel, and stare at buzzing gym lights high overhead.

"Lying down on the job?" Ms. Jameson's heels click across the gym floor. Brooke is at her side.

I hop up. "Yeah, well, no. Nobody showed up today."

"And they won't show up next week either. I just got off the phone with Maddie's mother. She pulled her daughter along with the rest. You no longer have a class."

"Why?" I kick at the mat. "I'm good at this."

"Which is why I agreed to let Brooke take a private lesson from you today. I know she'll be in good hands." Ms. Jameson turns to Brooke. "I'll leave you with your instructor."

Heeled shoes clop toward the door, which closes with a slam.

Brooke slips out of her warm-up pants, tosses them against the far wall. "I'm ready."

I don't move.

"Hey, I paid plenty for this." She runs her fingers over one shoulder and gently stretches her legs. Standing in that halter top and those shorts, she knows what she's doing.

She walks to the wall and strokes its surface. "What do you hold on to?"

I sigh, knowing she won't give up. "If you're gonna climb, you wear the harness." I size her, adjust it to her body, clip the clasp in front, and tie the rope. "I'll spot you from below. You can't fall. Reach with your hands, thrust upward with your legs."

"Reach. Thrust. Got it." She winks, and I chuckle.

Brooke steps up, slips. She re-places her foot, but falls awkwardly onto her rear.

"Can't fall, huh? I see why you like doing this." She

stands and winces and stares at me like it's my fault her coordination is crap. "Maybe you could help me a little?"

I reach my hands around her waist, feel her stomach tense and relax, and lift her onto the face. I press into her, pin her body while I stretch her hand to a solid grip. "You should be able to hold yourself up, now."

I pull away, and watch her arms shake. She's going down.

Brooke tumbles off the wall, makes like a housecat, and paws for my neck. She rings it, steadies herself. "This part isn't so bad." She bends forward, whispers, "I knew private lessons had benefits. There's a party at my house tonight." She runs her hand through my hair. "We could make that private, too."

I pry her loose, unhook her clasp, and turn. Salome stands on the far side of the gym.

"Salome!" I glance at Brooke. "No one showed up today."

Salome stares at Brooke and approaches.

"Hi, Salome." Brooke smiles, runs her hand across the back of my neck.

I squirm away and flatten my hair. "You stopped by." It's a dumb thing to say, but I'll do anything to wipe the devastated look off Salome's face.

Salome holds up her notebook. "I was studying in the library and thought I'd stop in. I wanted to see how your first day back went. Seems like it went fine."

"It did." Brooke tosses back her hair and smiles at me. "Jake taught me how to get started." She turns toward the wall. "It's harder than it looks."

Salome studies the pegs and the holes on the rock wall top to bottom. I know her. I know what she's thinking, the research she's doing. She's taking it apart, putting it together, like she does a story for the school paper. She's fighting that wall right now, and if she wins— *Oh, no.*

"Don't, Salome," I walk toward her, lower my voice. "You hate heights."

She stares at me; her mind's made up. "Is this what it takes?"

"What?"

She steps toward the wall, tosses her notebook next to Brooke's pants, and stretches her neck.

"You need the harness, Sal."

Salome reaches for a hold.

"The harness." I gesture to Brooke. "Take it off, now!"

Brooke fumbles with a strap and grins. "I'm having some problems here. Would you give me a hand?"

"Sal!"

She's up. Unwavering. She climbs straight up. No veering for the easy reach.

Brooke stares like I stare. "Did you teach her how to climb?"

"Nope." I shake my head. "That's all want-to."

Salome. If she were anyone else, I'd let my mind go where dreams have already been. I'd follow her up and meet her at the top. I'd gently touch her lips and her skin with trembling fingers. But I can't go there. It's a brutal type of can't. I can't lose her. The cracks she fills, the sense she makes, the hope she gives—all gone with one stupid touch.

Two minutes later she rings the victory bell, climbs over the top, and walks down. Salome is white, Brooke's red, and I feel a pukey yellow.

Salome grabs her notebook, brushes by me, and marches toward the exit. I lead Brooke off the mats, throw them in the corner, and chase Salome. I catch her outside. She turns the key to the Lees' Volvo, and I knock on the window. Salome puffs out air, and strands of hair around her face jump.

The window lowers slowly.

"Why'd you do that?" I ask. "You didn't need to do that."

She looks up to me. "You tell me what I need to do."

"To climb?" I reach in and squeeze her biceps. "I'd say you have that down. You should have seen Brooke fall on her butt."

She grabs my hand, pulls my arm in, and unloads on my shoulder.

I groan and pull out the deadened limb and watch the window raise on a happier face.

"What's that about?" I rub my arm and lean over her hood. We face each other through the windshield. I can't read her, and she's not talking.

"Okay, we'll do this not-answering thing. How about this one? You going to Brooke's party tonight?" I climb on top of the hood, stick my nose against the glass. "I bet it'll be big."

Wet squirts douse my face, and wiper blades catch me on the lips. Salome revs the car, throws it in reverse. I flop onto pavement, touch my mouth, and jump to my feet. "What's gotten into you?" I holler at the vanishing car.

I sweep the hair off my face and feel my shoulders slump.

Sal, it's for your own good. It's killing me, too.

CHAPTER 7

I DON'T KNOW ANYONE WHO likes Brooke.
She's drop-dead beautiful—she is that. And she knows
it—she's that, too. That explains why she makes boys
crazy and makes girls sick. But everyone, even Ellie,
her "best friend," spends a ton of time ripping her when
she's not around. Except on Friday nights. And especially when Julia, Brooke's mom, is on a Vegas run. Then
we all suck up, because parties at her house are insane.

Friday at Brooke's brings together the strangest as-
sortment of kids. Sportos and goths and drama geeks
and Immortal wannabes—kids who wouldn't glance at
each other outside the door of her gate drop it all and

live and let live inside. There's no explanation for it. It's a Brooke house thing.

I walk to Troy's place after dinner. He waits on his porch.

"You set?" I ask.

He jumps up. Strange seeing Troy again. Marriage and firefighting haven't changed him one bit. Cheyenne is still a hermit and seems cool with his going out, which is great for me.

I watch him approach and try to think of something not to like. No go. Troy smiles a lot and has no brain clouds. Life treats him good.

But maybe not now. He slows, and his gaze drops.

We walk past the mill. I stare at Dad's castle, where Troy's dad sweeps the floor.

Troy bends over, picks up a stone, and fires it toward the wooden gate. It bounces off the word *Hanking's* with a *thunk*. "My dad's still there, cleaning up your dad's mess."

I slow and replay his line. Very un-Troy. I speed up and say nothing.

Troy continues, "Monday after you were expelled, my dad got called in and reamed." He shoves me again. "Lectured on responsibility. Darn near fired. That should've been your lecture."

"Listen to you! Who was the one who ran away from high school after one year because of his *responsible* behavior with Cheyenne? Did her dad want to kill you because of your responsibility?"

I look up at Brooke's, a block in the distance, then back at my red-faced friend. I blink hard.

He glances over his shoulder. His voice softens. "I'm trying to do right by her, but—"

I get in his face, try to catch his gaze. "What's going on?"

"It's been tough lately." Troy eases down onto the curb. "Since we've been back, she's even quieter. It's like living in a morgue. Thought tonight might lighten the weight. At Brooke's." He leans back onto the grass. "But it's different. It's been too long, and walking to Brooke's feels different now." He exhales hard. "Cheyenne doesn't even want me to hang out with you anymore."

I think on that, nod.

"You aren't in high school anymore. Go home." I run my hand through my hair. "Cheyenne's great. There's nothing waiting at Brooke's that you don't have better at home."

He stares up at me, raises his eyebrows.

"Seriously," I say. "If I was hooked up with . . . Get

out of here." I step on his foot, wait for his groan, and leave him behind.

I reach Brooke's steps, where Salome and Kelli stand.

Salome looks around. "Troy didn't come with you?"

I point over my shoulder. "Is there still a body sprawled on the sidewalk?"

Kelli's mouth falls open. "Did you do that to him?"

"Yeah, just for fun. One right hook and—"

Salome boots my bad ankle, and I buckle.

"Troy!" She and Kelli push by me. I stand alone on the steps and picture the scene behind me. I hear Troy laugh. Salome joins him. I turn to wait for Salome and hear the door unlatch behind me.

"It's about time." Brooke grabs my forearm and yanks. It's her party, so I let her pull me in.

IT'S LOUD AND DIM, and the shadows of everyone I know are there—except Troy, who probably still lies on the sidewalk.

Feels strange to see kids from school, but I drag forward, hurtling by comments like I did trees down the mountain.

"Hey, Jake, whatcha been up to?"

"School's been a bore since you left."

"Salome was looking for you."

"What?" I pull against Brooke and strain to find the speaker.

"Let's go out back," Brooke hollers in my ear. "The hot tub was empty last time I checked." She pulls me through the house, onto the patio. The tub's not empty now.

Twenty kids sit around and laugh, and we move nearer, push through the crowd.

"Hey, brother." Scottie's narrow-eyed gaze wanders from me to Brooke. He pulls his arm free from the girl at his side. "You're not with Salome?"

Kyle and his brown leather jacket walk up from behind. "Forget her." He jams Scottie's head beneath the waterline. Two girls laugh and step out of the water, and the crowd cheers.

"Come on." Brooke pulls me off the patio, away from the pool, and behind the flower gardens.

"Listen, Brooke—"

"We don't need anyone else tonight." She reaches her arms around my neck and kisses me, hard and deep, but it takes me nowhere, and my mind wanders. To the hot tub, to the street, to Salome.

My hands move on instinct and reach for the buttons of her blouse.

There are two kinds of pretty. Brooke, she's part-time gorgeous—when you're with her, when her half-covered body drapes over yours. Right then, there's no doubt, she's something for the eyes. But Salome, she's pretty always—when you're at home and haven't seen her in days, or she won't talk to you. She's fill-the-brain pretty.

I let Brooke's blouse drop, and pause. She doesn't notice. Her hands grope, and her voice whispers my name, and this is the last place I want to be.

I pry her like a suction cup away from me, steady her at the shoulders. She blinks and cocks her head.

"It's okay. I'm okay with this." She lunges at me, and inside a switch flips. The dark cloud descends. I not only don't want her, I loathe her—loathe being near her. I push her away, reach down, and hand her the blouse.

"Put it on. I need to go."

I emerge from the flower garden to Salome and drippy Scottie. They stand close to where we were. Depending on the noise level, maybe they were too close. Maybe they heard.

"There you are." Salome reaches for my hand, looks me in the eyes, and pauses. "Oh, tell me no."

"No! Nothing," I say. "I stopped."

Brooke runs out, hands clutched around the top

pressed against her. "Oh, hi, Scottie, Salome." She turns to me. "Guess everyone is looking for you."

"I—I need to go." I push out of this gruesome party and toward the gate.

SALOME SPENDS SATURDAY locked away at home, where she doesn't take my calls and destroys my weekend.

I spend the day in the garage, sharpening saw blades and staring at my jacket shred. Maybe it is cursed, but it brings me comfort. I set down my blades, work the leather, and wander onto the driveway. She can see me clearly from there. I whistle, wander back beside the truck, and repeat the process.

I gaze into her window, see her shape, and glance away.

Come out here. Let me explain.

But she doesn't, and after thirty trips down to the mailbox, I quit. I head inside, slam the garage door behind me. I won't see her tomorrow either—she'll be rolling away at Brockton Baptist—morning service and afternoon meetings and evening service. It's awful having God as your competition.

Monday arrives, and I haven't seen her in three days. There's a buzzy jitter inside, one only she can calm.

I hop on my scooter and whiz down Winders Street through a semideserted world. The kids are locked up in school, their parents are incarcerated in the mill, I'm under house arrest—tough town.

I accelerate and pull into the high school parking lot and check my watch. Third hour. Phys ed. Perfect. I walk the perimeter of the campus and reach the ballfields on the far side. Across the football field, twenty girls jog the track. Well, four jog and about sixteen walk.

I stick to the tree line that skirts the field and smile. Salome runs. Of course she runs. I slip under the bleachers and work my way down to the middle of the track. I crawl forward, squeeze up through a crack, and plunk down on the metal seat, hands folded.

Salome, Kelli, and Haley jog the far side, circle round toward me. Walkers stare as they pass—or giggle or shake their heads or start to jog—but what they say or do doesn't matter. It's only the blonde who wears my red PROPERTY OF sweatshirt, the one who laughs free and clear. I see her, and the tingle stops. And a different type of tingle starts.

"Jake! What are you doing here?" She pulls up with Haley. They lean over the fence, while Kelli mutters and runs on.

"Thought I'd visit, is all."

"You can't be here." Salome says.

Haley gazes around the track and glances all nervous like at the school, as if some drug deal is going down. "If they see you here, you'll be—"

"Suspended? Expelled?" I ask.

"Honestly, Jake." Salome runs her hand through her hair. "What do you need?"

"You," I say.

Haley smiles and starts to run. Salome climbs the fence, sits down next to me.

"What do you mean by that?"

"Where's Mrs. Hurd?" I ask.

"She's not here today. We have a seriously obese sub watching us run from the building." She bites her lip. "What did you mean by that?"

"What?" I ask.

"You."

"You?"

She fists my thigh. "That's what you said. 'You'! I asked you what you needed, and you said 'you'!"

"Then I said it wrong, 'cause I didn't mean me, I meant to say y—"

Salome leans forward, hugs her legs. "How old are you?"

"Eight."

"Eight. Well, that explains everything." She stands, steps down, and jumps back onto the track. "We aren't in third grade. Things can change. You know that."

"I know. Like now? You look damn pretty in my sweatshirt."

She stands there, shoulders hanging, mouth partly open. Like I screwed up. Like she doesn't want my compliment.

I rise and walk down to the fence. "I meant that you look great." Her face hasn't twitched. "You know, compared to all of them." I point.

"I need to go." Salome backs away. "I really need to go right now."

"Come over later," I call after her. "When you disappear on me for a weekend, it gets tough."

I stand at the fence and watch. Kelli and Haley make it around the track and slow when they reach her. Salome doesn't look at them. Soon Kelli throws an arm around Salome and stares at me. Dagger stares. You-better-be-gone-by-the-time-we-get-around-this-track stares.

I stand and leave. I feel better, but I know something got worse.

CHAPTER 8

AT HANKING'S, MONDAY IS discard day—
when odd-shaped wood hunks pile up behind the
mill—so I scoot home by way of Dad's empire. I
scrounge through pallets and twisted boards. Dad's
castoffs.

I find twenty planks, busted and worn. Perfect for
extending my landing ramp. I load them into a Hanking's truck and drive over to the irregular lumber pile. I
feel my eyes light. It's a gold mine.

I pitch planks and timbers onto the truck bed.

*Something's not right. These pieces are too good. They
pulverize and pulpify this stuff.*

My gut flutters. *Something happened to Dad. He wouldn't let this get by.*

I finish loading and climb the back stairway that leads to his office. Inside, muffled voices. Dad's letting someone have it. I scrape sawdust from the window with the heel of my hand and see the victim the same moment he sees me. Scottie.

My brother races toward the door, throws it open, and yanks me inside.

"He's got nothing to do with this." Dad stares at me like I want to be here, as if I've been standing outside with a number.

"It's all of us, Dad." He's got me by the shoulders, a human shield that he pushes at Dad on every emphasized word. "Every firefighter in Brockton. This is about all of us."

"Your brother isn't one of us." Dad says quietly.

His words pierce deep, and I feel weak, breathless.

"But someday he might be, and Kyle said that Mox—"

"Moxie Stone is the bravest man I've ever met. I knew him when he was first picked up. I fought beside him when you were three, and he wasn't more than a rookie. He saved me countless times, when I was younger and stupider and thought life was a game like—" Dad glances at me, and his voice calms. "What have you got against him? And what does he have to do with Kyle? Mox is in Montana, Scottie!"

"I know, Dad. And I don't understand it all. I'm on the hand crew, Kyle's on Mox's rappel crew, so I don't know it all. But a friend warned me about that jacket, and I didn't take it. Then Mox's crew offered it to Kyle, and he did. He barely recovered from the accident, and now he's terrified and keeps saying he's going to die." Scottie curses. "My best friend won't tell me what is going on. That's not right. Something's not right. And you know how many good young firefighters we've lost."

Dad is silent. He folds his arms, big and meaty.

"For once, just once, don't make me earn this," Scottie says. "Just believe me that, beneath all the good we do, there's something real evil, and Kyle's messed up in it. He called it the club and said it involves the Immortals from all different crews and Mox runs this thing." He squeezes my arms hard. "Don't you ever wonder why Immortals stick around all year? Why they never leave Brockton?"

"Dedication."

"Initiation." Scottie's voice quavers. "Year-round initiations."

"You're asking me to choose between your half information and my own gut." Dad nods and stares out the window. "Thirty-eight years fighting blazes—my gut is why I'm still alive. You're just a boy."

Silence. Scottie releases my shoulders and turns. I look from Dad to my brother. Their backs are turned, and they don't budge, and it seems a good time to leave.

"If you two don't mind, I'm gonna—"

Dad flings his arm toward me, shoos me like a fly. "Go on back to your trash heap."

I snap, as certain and permanent as bone, and I want to smack him.

Scottie reaches out and grabs my shoulder. I pull away, and he grabs again, and hugs me, hard and real.

I go weak and lower my head onto his shoulder. Whenever I see a group part for Scottie, hear them shut up when he opens his mouth, my chest wants to burst. That's *my* brother. The brilliant one. Scottie's the right look and the right word at the right time. Always. But I hate him. I have to hate him, 'cause if I don't, I'll shrivel up and die.

I lift up my head and tense until he lets go.

"Go home, Jake." Dad nods toward the door. "Scottie and I need to finish this."

I back out and pound down metal steps. I don't know

what's happening in there, but I can't be near it.

I drive my treasure into the mountains, heap the scraps next to the ramp, and pound planks into place.

The club full of Immortals. My kind of place.

But soon the sky opens. I wrap my tools as rain falls in sheets, and I slowly wind down toward home.

I pull in the drive, walk toward the door. It doesn't feel right.

Above me, a crash. The barrel of Scottie's bat smashes out the bedroom window and shards of glass rain onto the lawn beside me.

I slowly push inside.

Dad calmly walks by, says nothing.

I reach for his arm. "Why is Scottie—"

Another crash from upstairs, and Dad pauses, stares at the floor. He turns, his eyes glazed and his voice a monotone. "The body was facedown, floating in the caves."

The most terrifying scream fills the house—nonhuman, filled with emotions I don't know. But it is human. It's Scottie. And I want to run, toward him, away from him, just run.

Dad swallows hard, rubs his face with his hand, and tells me the only thing I don't want to know.

"It was Kyle."

CHAPTER 9

I CAN'T SLEEP.

One day Kyle's walking into my house; the next he's bloated and dead.

I get out of bed, step out of my room, and walk down the hall. Mom's flower-print chair, the only remnant of her left in the house, faces out the oversize window. I sink into the cushion, put up my feet, and stare out. It's dark at Salome's—a safe dark.

I run fingers along the radiator and pause. I've reached the spot rubbed gray, where no white paint remains. Where ten-year-old hands once tied quick knots out of bedsheets. It was a fast rappel down the side of the house and a race across Salome's yard, and it was worth it.

"How did you get up here, Jake?"

"I slid down the sheets and climbed up your bricks. Wanna come out?"

"It's ten, no, it's eleven o'clock, and if Mom checks on me . . ." She stares out her window. "How do you climb bricks?"

"Fast. You have to move fast."

"You have to leave fast. I think Mom'll be mad."

"Yeah, okay. I just wanted to say good night."

"You came all the way over to say good night?"

I nod my head.

"That's nice."

I scamper down, run home, and pull myself up the sheets, arm over arm. Salome is still watching. I know she is, and I want to make sure she sees how strong I am.

The moon shines full, and I rise. "Good night, Salome. I . . . will see you tomorrow." I amble toward my room and freeze. Light glimmers from beneath Scottie's door, and I turn the knob, peek in.

He places clothes into a suitcase: no duffel stuffing like when Dad was called to a blaze fire. These shirts go in slow and calculated.

"Shut the door."

"With me inside or outside?"

He straightens, exhales, and gestures toward the desk chair with his head. I quietly slip in, close the door, sit down, and wait.

"Are you just going to watch?" Scottie turns to me and stares, as if he's looking for something.

I shrug. "Okay, I'll bite. Where are you going?"

Scottie snaps shut the suitcase and sets it beside the duffel on the floor. "I need to leave here. I know something I shouldn't." He raises his gaze to me. "I need to take care of it."

"And you have to leave home to do it?"

"I need to leave everything to do it."

We look at each other for a long time. He's still here, and I miss him already. I miss his jerky big-brother act and that stupid poker face.

"Are you coming back?" I ask.

He looks down.

I nod. "Sorry about Kyle."

"What do you care?" he hisses, runs his hand through his hair. He closes his eyes. "It's not your fault anyway. It's mine. All mine."

"I'm the one who hurt him."

"I'm the one who killed him."

I frown and lick my lips.

Scottie walks toward me, reaches down, yanks me up by the shoulders. He hugs me hard. Twice he's done this, ever, and both within a day. But this one is different. There's no Dad here, and the hug feels better than good. I don't know why he's squeezing me or why I squeeze him back, but it's right.

He pushes back. "I don't understand you. Your wild crap doesn't make any sense, especially when you have Salome. You have the world, and you keep risking it all."

I bite my lip hard. "Nobody has Sal."

Scottie picks up his bags, lets out air. "Tell Dad I was looking forward to fighting in Brockton."

I've dreamed of this day. The day my brother leaves and maybe I exist. But now, holding the moment in my hand, I feel sick. "So you won't tell me where—"

"Forest Service headquarters. I need to talk to them, turn in my gear. Then, who knows, maybe I'll go see Mom."

"You're quitting?" My knees weaken. "Dad'll freak. You're leaving me alone with him?"

He leans into me. "You'll be fine. Stay close to Sal, and you'll be fine." Scottie frowns. "Where is that cursed scrap of leather?"

"My room."

"Get it."

I leave and come back carrying my jacket. He grabs it from my hands, drops his suitcase, clicks it back open, and stuffs it in.

"You're stealing my jacket."

"I'm saving your life."

He lifts his suitcase, and together we walk into the night.

We load his truck, he climbs in, and the Chev rumbles to life. "Promise me something?"

"A guarantee."

"Stay away from the Fire Service. And stay away from Mox."

"Why?"

He locks on to me. "Because they'll be after you, and even you aren't immortal."

CHAPTER 10

DEATH HITS BROCKTON HARD. Usually the
town shakes it off, but this death smacked it between the
eyes, stayed the talk of the town for days, not hours.

Scottie's "death," that is.

The town's favorite son is gone.

Dad doesn't go to the mill for a week. He puts
on a good face, nods and smiles whenever an old
firefighter buddy comes to call. I listen to Dad talk.
I hear him explain that firefighting wasn't right for
Scottie, but then comes silence, followed by a bar-
rage of questions he can't answer.

Why are Brockton's crews under investigation? Why

do the feds keep showing up in town? Why all the interviews with the Immortals?

The door slams, and Dad blows. "It's not my fault. This wasn't my fault."

But the truth is, he's embarrassed and pissed and blames me for the whole thing.

You could have got me out of bed!

And the most insane:

Your craziness finally rubbed off on him.

Salome and I move our talks to the train depot at town's edge.

"Has he spoken to you yet?" Salome swings her legs, looks up from the empty boxcar.

"No. He mumbles a lot, but not to me. He emptied Scottie's room—no sign of him left anywhere."

Salome leans back. "I, uh, I got a sign. He called me last night."

I leap off the depot roof and land on the platform. Ankles scream. I wince and hobble toward her.

"He asked how you were doing." She stares straight ahead, her voice quiet.

"Why'd he call you?"

Salome shrugs, hops out, and reaches for my hand. She pulls me onto the tracks. "Let's head back."

"Why'd he call you?"

We each balance on a rail and head into town. Her hand reassures, but my mind is rough.

She swings my arm and slips off the rail, steps back on.

"Your little school visit the other day got people talking again," she says.

"You didn't tell me why Scottie called—wait, talking 'bout what?"

Her arm stops swinging. I start the pendulum again.

"Why *did* you show up at school?" she asks.

"Hard to explain." I blink hard. "You know the jittery thing. Your voice calms it down, is all." I peek toward her. "Right answer?"

She nods slowly, and we walk in silence.

"Are you there?" I ask.

"I heard from the School of Journalism at Mid Cal. Orientation is June 2. I start June 10."

Lungs burn, and that ripping sensation works right down my middle, neck to gut.

"And you're still thinking four years?"

"It's a four-year program. I can't believe it's coming true. It's what I do well." She squeezes my hand.

It's quiet for a long time.

"It'll suck here." I slow. "You talked about leaving, but it was just out there, ya know? Now it's . . ."

Salome tugs. My turn to fall off the rail. She joins me in the middle, and we face each other square. "Do you suddenly not want me to go?"

"Space. Too much of it between you and me."

We stand a foot apart. Her lips curl up on the left, like they always do before she smiles. But she does not smile. Her lips remain, and her eyes widen into a face I've not seen and can't resist long, not from this close.

My gaze travels her face, drops to her shoulder, and follows the curve of her elbow down to her waist. My fingertips tingle. They want to surround that waist, draw her in.

But the world would stop spinning and I'd lose the best piece of me and she'd end up in pieces. I know that like I know my name.

I exhale. "I mean, shouldn't best friends stay together?"

Her curl vanishes, and she steps back. "Nothing changes for you. If you had it your way, we'd be neighbors until we're ninety-nine!"

I puff out more air and stare at a beautiful girl who couldn't be more wrong.

"You know, you're right. I think it's an awesome deal, and absolutely you should go." I turn and walk forward. She doesn't come with me.

I peek back at her. Salome hangs her head.

"Come on." I reach out my hand. She stares at it and takes it.

But she's thinking. Still thinking hard. Probably a God comment fighting to get out, but I don't want it, and she knows it.

I breathe deep. Dad's got it right. Suckin' air is all I'm doing. No diploma. No nothing. Salome's got a chance. She swings my arm. Even when sad, her face shines light and free. She's breathing in a different kind of oxygen.

Salome stops and steps across the rails. "Scottie's with your mom."

Whoosh. Brain cloud gone. Completely. I blink, tingle, blink again.

"When he left, he said he might go see her, but he hates her. Didn't think he'd actually go. He never returns her letters, deletes her e-mails." I reach down for a rock, stand, and whip it down the tracks. "How long is he staying with her?"

"He wouldn't say."

Inky black returns. Scottie with Mom. Monkey Boy with Dad. Unbelievable.

We leave the tracks we're supposed to follow, finish our walk in silence, and turn up our street. From behind, tires squeal, and a beat-up station wagon chirps to a stop beside us. The window rolls down. Salome grabs my forearm and squeezes.

"Where's your brother, Jake?" Mox stares at me. "Where's your snake of a brother?"

Moxie Stone is twice my age, and his voice rumbles deep and hypnotic. When he talks, people do. He's the nearest thing to a firefighting legend there is, and his appearance in Brockton normally marks the beginning of wildfire season. But he's early. Way early. Men revere him. If half the stories of his heli-rappelling heroism are true, I should get on my knees. But he ripped my brother, and only I get to do that.

I lean into his window and whisper, "I don't know where he is. Find him yourself."

He grabs my shirt, his face emotionless. He looks at me; I stare back. Not at him. His jacket. The brown one with the *I* across the shoulders.

"Let go of him, you jerk!" Salome says.

Mox glances at her, an ugly up-and-down glance, and releases me. "Drew's sister is all grown up." He shoves my head out of the car and accelerates toward my home. Salome and I run. Dad's a mess and Mox is hot, and we better get there before he does.

We cut through yards. I boost Salome over Harry's

privacy fence, then pull myself up to the top. We bolt across two cross streets, wind breathless up the hill, and pull up on my driveway.

Mox and Dad already talk on the step. Both glance at me and go back to their conversation.

"So he's done, then," Mox says.

Dad hangs his head and nods. "I don't understand. It was going so well, then all this nonsense about you and some doomsday club—"

Mox's fingers flex and fist. He reaches up and gives his forehead a good rub.

"You can only do so much with kids. They have their own minds, right?" Mox peeks at me over his shoulder. "They'll get an idea, make up a story."

"Scottie wasn't like that." Dad shakes his head. "He never made up anything. Different than—" He gestures toward me with his head.

"Well." Mox gives Dad a firm pat to the shoulder. "He was a great son, and would have been a great asset to Brockton. We'll all miss him."

Dad looks up. He straightens for the first time in weeks.

"Who knows, in a few years, maybe the other one will pick up the ax," Mox says.

"Maybe sooner . . . listen, you'll never find Jake's

equal in strength, and I'm telling you he's fearless." He leans forward. "Fearless."

Dad lowers his voice to a level I'm still meant to hear. "I took the liberty of making a few calls—"

Mox stiffens. "Tell me right now this isn't going where I think it is."

"Kyle's tragedy leaves you a man short. Now, I know Jake hasn't trained, but I spoke with Richie, and that will not be a problem. He is short on experience. But he should be dead given all the crazy stunts he's pulled."

"I choose my men."

"And he *will* be dead if he doesn't come under some discipline."

"*I* choose my men!"

"And so the chief is considering a temporary arrangement—"

Mox turns and glares at me. Salome grabs my sleeve.

Dad places his hand on Mox's shoulder. "Jake's a tough, strong kid. Maybe he'll make me proud yet."

"Ignore them, Jake. Remember what happened to Kyle, to Drew? A few weeks on Mox's crew, and they were gone." Salome yanks me toward her house. "This has nothing to do with you."

She's wrong. She doesn't know what falling down a

line into a blaze would do. Surrounded by flames. It'd be like Hades. Then to be pulled out? That's flippin' biblical-like intensity. A resurrection.

But Mox doesn't want me. And Dad is the one who dangled this carrot, which means I can't take it.

I kick at the ground, salivate, and let my body fall away with Salome.

We reach her front door.

"What are you thinking, Jake?"

I turn back toward my place and watch Mox's wagon speed off.

"That I came that close to getting a jacket."

CHAPTER 11

I TOOH THE LIBERTY of making a few calls.

Dad's words carry me to Hanking's and push me into a truck. They press my foot against the accelerator and speed me toward my dump. They push me through the woods, into the salvage yard, and onto my dirt bike.

Like I'll ever have a chance at Mox's team or a jacket now.

I rev the engine.

Selling me to Mox like I was a piece of meat.

I crank the accelerator, kick up a plume of dust.

Here's a strong one for ya, Mox.

More dust surrounds me.

Fearless. Absolutely fearless.

The engine fires.

"Yah!" I squeal forward, pull a tight circle around the cars, and line up in front of my takeoff ramp. Someday I might have signed on if Dad'd kept his fat hands out of it.

I rev and chirp forward. Faster and faster over the dirt. Wheels hit wood, my body lifts, and I'm weightless. I squeeze the grips, lift the front end, and the bottom falls out of the jump.

I'm going down.

Crash. My rear tire catches on the water heater, and I fly over the handlebars. I ball up and land hard on wood; my body flops and rolls over and skids to a stop in the dirt.

My ears ring and I fight for air, but I can think. Clear as clear. I'm alive.

In time, the ringing lessens, and somewhere a bird chirps. Then another. Slowly, the sounds of the forest return. I lie motionless and stare at my toes. They move, they feel. The legs and hips as well. I reach my head. Unbelievable. Everything hurts, but nothing's broken.

It takes minutes to stand. More still to hobble toward what was my bike. I look at it twisted in the dirt.

I shake my head and lug it toward the road. The bike

will need serious surgery in my garage. I fight it onto the truck bed, and ease into the cab.

It's a slow drive down to Brockton. I park the Ford beside the fleet in Hanking's lot. I push out of the cab, grimace, and work my way toward the truck bed.

"Heard from your weasel brother?"

I squint toward the street.

Dale and Will, fresh up from Albuquerque, talk over a parked car in the street. "Well?" Dale calls.

"Uh—"

Dad leans out of the office door and motions me up. "I need you up here, Jake."

I peek back toward the street, and Will starts a rhythmic kick of his tire.

"I'm comin' right up! I just have something down here to finish."

I turn toward Dale. "Why did you call him a weasel?"

"I'll tell you why." He starts across the street. Will grabs his forearm from behind.

"Jake's clueless. Let it go."

Dale stops, stretches his neck from side to side. He exhales hard. "You wouldn't understand anyway."

"Jake. Now!"

Dad is hot, and I'm sick of being caught in between. I backpedal toward the stairs and grab the rail. Climbing is miserable on my legs, but I reach the top and follow him inside. He looks me up and down but says nothing.

He leads me out his office door, and we stand shoulder to shoulder, looking down over his pack rats. It's Dad's term, but it seems to fit. They scurry around the mill, pause to peek at me and purse their lips, before lowering hard hats and hauling lumber into the yard. Today, the mill is bigger than I remember and less a place I recognize.

"You're eighteen now, nearing nineteen," Dad says.

"You're fifty-six."

"There's a lot of life left for you. Lots of time to make things right."

Hairs on my neck bristle, and I inch away. "Maybe. But maybe not in Brockton. Scottie left. Salome's leaving. I'm thinking I should, too."

Dad's fists clench the rail.

I tap my foot and think hard of something to say. "How's Mr. Ramirez holdin' up?"

Dad doesn't answer. He just stares across the mill, his face expressionless.

"Mr. King?" Julia, one of Dad's most underdressed employees, places her hand on Dad's neck and rubs.

So that's where Brooke got that. Like mother, like daughter.

"Could I get a signature?" she asks.

Dad doesn't look at the clipboard—he just scribbles.

"Well, what's the town nut been up to? You look terrible." She cocks her head and gives a saccharin smile.

Dad shakes—a whole body tremble—and Julia steps back. He grabs the clipboard from her hand, cracks it in half over his leg, and throws it down behind him. Julia freezes. I do, too.

"Pack up your things and leave." Dad stares at Julia and points toward her office. "You're done here."

She steps forward, eyebrows raised, makeup cracking all over her face. Her voice is quiet. "But the way you've been talking, I thought—"

"This is my son," he says quietly. "And you're my ex-employee."

I don't get it. I don't understand him—how in the same breath he can destroy and defend me.

I enter his office and plop into a chair. Behind me, the door quietly shuts. Dad takes his seat.

I exhale hard. "Julia didn't say anything that terrible."

"You're all I've got left." He rubs his face hard. "You asked about Kyle's dad. He's still taking it tough. A man losing two sons to stupidity is more than any man can bear. He's never gotten over Carter."

It's my turn to rub my face. You don't forget people

jumping trains with four-wheelers or floating facedown in caves.

Dad whispers, "Like they're playing video games. These stupid kids."

I look at Dad. His eyes glisten.

"Why do you do it? What makes a boy like Carter do that?"

"Plenty of people think it's Mox. They think those jackets are the kiss of death." My eyes grow big. "Since Drew, that's what Salome thinks."

"Not her, too. Scottie and Salome—will you please tell me what Mox did to deserve all these rumors?"

"Hey, I said nothing about the man." I lean forward. "What did Scottie tell you about him?"

Dad shakes his head. Conversation over.

I check my watch. "Are we done? I've had a tough day, and I have a sick dirt bike that needs me."

He sniffs and looks at me. "What do *you* think about the Forest Service . . . specifically Mox's team?"

"You're asking me what *I* want?"

"You could do something good for this town," he continues. "And for me."

I look off toward the window and whisper, "I'm not Scottie."

"No, you're not."

"And Mox made it clear he doesn't want to see me."

"True again. But what else do you have?" Dad leans forward. "Here's the deal. You're still under my roof." He raises his hand and lifts two fingers. "I'm giving you two choices for the rest of the year. Work at the mill." He looks out the window. "Heck, you can have Julia's job. Or get your fire training and prove to Mox and Brockton that he's pegged you wrong."

I stare back. "Has he?" Dad leans back slowly, and I continue. "I'm sure cutting brush was a thrill for you, but it takes a lot more for me."

"I know." He pushes back from the desk and stands. "So now, tragically, there's an opening on Mox's team for a rappeller. I thought dropping out of a helicopter might suit. I did make some calls. I did open the door for you. Richardson is willing to consider it. Do you want it?" Dad lowers his gaze and smiles. It's a strange grin. I-know-something and I'd-be-proud all wrapped up together.

"You're giving me a choice?" I run both hands through my hair. "You could really get me in? Even over Mox?"

He shrugs. "Possible." Dad walks toward the door, yawns and stretches. "Thought I'd let you know." He starts to whistle and walks out of the room. Slimy trickster. He knows he has me.

I BURST INTO THE BROCHTON Library, race up to Ethel at the info desk. She smacks her gum and checks bright red nails and gabs about the spa on her cell.

A minute of finger drumming later, she peeks at me and tongues the inside of her cheek.

"Just one minute, Frances." She covers the mouth-piece and raises both eyebrows.

"I need to talk to—"

"Conference room two." She leans forward and slaps her hand on mine. "I didn't tell you."

"Thanks!" I cruise past her, around the corner, and throw open the door.

"You'll never guess what just opened up for—"

Salome stands; six others don't look too pleased.

Mr. Keating, advisor to the school paper, lowers his head and adjusts his glasses on their perch on the tip of his nose. "Another accident, I presume."

I nod and peek at Salome. My grin even feels goofy. "You're a good presumer."

Chris Rollins, a hyperactive junior, grabs his pen and starts scribbling my quote on his pad.

Mr. K. rolls his eyes, taps his watch and sighs. "Two minutes, Salome."

She hurries out, shuts the door behind her. "You better have a good one. 'Evolution Debunked!' or 'Brockton High Attacked by Killer Bees' or—"

"How about, 'Town Idiot Gets Shot at Redemption from Most Unlikely Source.'"

She scrunches her nose. "I like it. Punchy. And the subtitle?"

"'Jake Finally Comes to His Senses.'"

Salome stares at me and bites her lip gently. "I'll read on. Killer lead?"

I scratch my head. "Let's see. For too many years, Jake King, aka idiot, has fought against the undeniable, ignoring what stood right in front of him."

Salome lowers her pad. "If you're making this up, Jake, you stop right here."

"Take it to the press. I'll even give you another source so you can check my story. Dad."

"You told your dad how you feel?" Her eyes grow big, sparkle like they haven't in months.

"Come to think of it, he's probably been onto this story a long time."

The door opens behind her and Mr. K. pops his head

out. "We need you back in here. We're discussing your prom-styles piece."

"Working on it right now," she says, pushes the door shut with her foot.

She puts her arms on my shoulders and steps way close. "Read me the last paragraph. Read it slow, and read it clear."

I grab her waist and watch her eyes twinkle. She's so pumped for me.

"I've settled it in here." I point to my head. "I belong on Mox's rappelling crew."

CHAPTER 12

ROCHFORD. Three hundred miles due north. Five hours to fed headquarters.

It's plenty of time to think over my talk with Salome three days previous. I replay the interchange over and over. Her excitement. Her twinkle. Our embrace.

Her slap across my cheek before she silently exited the library.

Of course, she hates this: she already thinks Mox stole her brother. But I'm not like Drew. He was great, but I'm not like him. I'm not cautious or calculated, and I'm not fighting fire because it's noble.

I need it to live.

I reach Rockford. I've been driving since five A.M., and I'm beat. They could have rejected me on the phone, but Chief Richardson wouldn't say anything, so I still have a glint of hope.

I park my Beetle, step out into California heat, and rub my eyes. I sigh and walk across the brown front lawn in front of the administration building.

I push inside and glance around. Pictures of blazes taken from inside the infernos blanket the walls. Each photo holds a hero, a firefighter midyell, racing toward a nightmare that everyone else flees. And as I stand, my jaw tightens and I straighten. I want this like I can't remember wanting anything else. That's me in those pictures. It needs to be me.

I turn toward the lobby and the four reclining men who own it. They joke and laugh like we're at a comedy club. Mox reclines on the end, quiets when he sees me. They size me up, and I hate it.

Mox is the leader of this group, I know that much. He stares at me from within his brown jacket.

I peer at him and watch his face change. It hardens. Laughter turns to rage in moments. It's like Mr. Ramirez turning from Salome to me. He hates me.

"Richardson's through that door." Mox nods. "You're late."

I frown, then turn and knock firmly.

From inside, a cheery voice. "It's open."

I enter slowly. Three men seated at a round table. One empty chair.

"Sit down, Jake." Richardson leans back, folds his arms across his tremendous gut.

I nod and take a seat.

All three men slip rubber bands off thick manila folders. "We want you, Jake," Richardson continues, opens the first page, and sighs. "But I'll be straight. We don't want you *now*. You have no business on a hotshot heli-rappeling crew. With no experience, you'd be nothing but a liability."

I think of the photo gallery in the lobby, and my gut sinks. I don't get it. "So that's it." I push back from the desk.

"Hold on, kid. Hank made quite a case. I thought I'd at least take a look at where you might belong. Here's what I found. Let's see." He adjusts his rims. "Willful property destruction, reckless endangerment . . ." He glances at the others. "There's an irony for you, gentlemen." He clears his throat. "Where was I? Let's see, reckless endangerment, theft—" Richardson flips through several more papers. "Shoot, none of this makes us blink. We have whole inmate firefighting crews."

"So you *do* want me?"

"Wanting and accepting are different matters. Let me ask you, do you want to be a rappeller?"

"Yeah." I rub my face. "Bad."

Chief Richardson leans back, and his chair creaks. "I won't lie to you. I owe your father more favors than I've got fingers. He's been pushing hard for me to waive your two-year fighting-experience prerequisite." He exhales long and loud. "That's pushing the bounds of sanity. You'll hold men's lives in your hands.

"But Hank's put me in a spot. He wants you with Mox, who I think would rather jam his hand in a hornets' nest."

I nod.

"I've called you up to say I will push this through, based on your next few months of training performance and whether you can satisfy one of our concerns."

"Just one?" I crane my neck to see his folder.

Richardson reads something, lets out a loud blast of air, taps his own head. "In here." He slams the folder shut. "I got a list a mile long of crazy stunts you've pulled. Firing bottle rockets off the top of your school." He smiles and wags his head. "In kindergarten? Geez, Jake."

I bite my lip. "Can I see that list?"

"We don't care about that. But we can't send you out if the mind's not right."

I shift in my chair.

"The fighter on your stick will put his life in your green hands." The thin man with the thin frames massages the divot on his nose. "Your brother only lasted in Brockton two weeks. Good thing, too. It was a good thing he snapped off-season. There's no place out there to make this personal."

I breathe deep.

"And there's this other matter of what you've described as a 'brain cloud.'" Richardson looks worried. "Have you ever thought of suicide?"

I force my hand through my hair. I haven't talked to Dad about the fogginess for years. "Where did you get all this—"

"What's a brain cloud, Jake?"

It breaks. All my posturing breaks, and my body goes limp. I slump down in my chair. "It's like a confusion, you know? It's on me most all the time. One big brain fog. And I think, why am I here?"

I peek up. They look at one another.

"Except when I'm pumped up. Like when I'm

climbing or free-falling—Salome says I'm an adrenaline junkie." I chuckle. "She knows me better than anyone."

I want to see her. Now. But I have to finish. "When that burst of adrenaline comes, the cloud goes, and I feel alive. I'm totally here, right? I focus and feel normal, and that's one reason why this job is perfect for me."

I need Salome. She always bursts in and makes it right, makes me right. She's been doing that since elementary school. I close my eyes and remember.

"ADHD. E/BD. Oppositional Defiant Disorder. There's no place here for Jake."

I stare down at rope-burned hands, the ones that climbed the gym rope, reached for the protective grate, and monkey-barred across the gym ceiling to a small windowsill.

"You're a school," Mom says, "My son is eight years—"

Principal Haynes stands, walks around his desk, and bends down. He stares at me.

"When we must call the fire department to rescue your son from our gymnasium, we no longer provide the services he needs."

I glance at Mom. Her hands shake. They always shake. I want to get her to the pottery wheel, the one that makes me dizzy and calms her down. She can't defend me, not alone. Haynes, like everyone else, thinks she's crazy.

She whispers through tears, "Where does my son be-long?"

The principal stands. "There are facilities."

"What's he talking about?" I ask.

"Special school," Mom whispers.

I nod. "Can I go to lunch now?"

Principal Haynes shakes his head. "The boy has no idea what's going on—"

I push back my chair. "You want to get rid of me. You don't want to see me again."

"That's not true, young man—"

The door opens. Salome.

"Excuse me— Oh, hi, Mrs. King!"

"Hello, dear."

"Hey, Jake. You didn't tell him, did you?" Salome's hands raise to her hips, and she taps her foot.

I say nothing.

"You need to be in the lunchroom, Salome." Haynes points out the door. "Now, please."

"Not until he tells you why he climbed. Not until he tells you that Kevin whipped my locket onto the sill above the gym. I'm not leaving until he tells you that he was climbing to get the gold locket my brother bought me, be-cause Mr. Jenkins wouldn't call the custodian to do it."

She looks at me. "When he tells you that, then I'll leave."

The principal frowns and looks from her to me. "Is that so?"

I dig in my pocket, bring out her heart locket, and hand it to her. "You can leave now." I smile, and she does, too.

My eyelids flutter open. She's not here, and I stare down at the table and listen to the buzz of fluorescent lights. After they deny me, I have nowhere to go. Finally, Richardson clears his throat.

"Where's this Salome?"

"Now? Brockton. Mid-Cal State in June."

"Does she matter to you, son?"

I exhale long and loud and stare at ceiling tiles.

"Good. Never had a problem with a man who cares for a woman." All three of them rise. "Welcome to training, Jake." Chief hikes up his pants. "You survive it, and we'll talk about a probationary period on Mox's crew."

I frown. "It's just a few weeks of helicopter stuff and a couple push-ups, right?"

Richardson clears his throat. "Maybe in Brockton. That would be the rappeller training you'd get. But you're not training in Brockton. You'll be in Herndon."

"Herndon? That's a smoke-jumping base."

"Yes, and I've told them to push you as hard as they

can through the two-month ordeal. If you survive that, I'll feel much better about this little arrangement. Wait here." Richardson slaps my back. "I'll ask Mox to come in."

They leave, and I slump down into my chair, a mile-long grin on my face.

Smoke jumpers. Jumping out of airplanes.

Ten minutes later, I pace the room. Finally, Mox slips in. He closes the door and flicks off the light. The pale red glow from the exit sign does little, and we stare into darkness.

"What frightens you, Jake?"

"Nothing."

"Dying? Are you afraid of death?"

"No."

"How about losing your family?"

"No. Pretty much lost them already."

"Tell me about Scottie." Mox whispers. "Where'd he end up?"

"My— No idea. I don't care."

Mox breathes hard. "Are you two close?"

"Turn on the light. I'm too old for ghost stories."

"Are you? Tell me about Salome Lee."

"You already know who she is. There's nothing to tell."

"Is she your girlfriend?"

I walk toward Mox. "There's nothing to tell."

"Are you afraid of losing her?"

I pause, then say the first uncomfortable thing in this conversation. "Yes."

I feel his breath. A hand grabs my shirt, balls it tight. "Jake King, I hate this. I hate you here. It's everything I fight against. Underprepared. Untested. I hate you on my crew. But this isn't your fault. So I'm giving you some advice: flunk out of training." His voice lowers. "Or bug out now like your brother. Because I didn't pull your cert, and life on my crew won't be pleasant."

He flicks on the lights, and I squint and blink.

"Sorry about the eyes. I focus better in the dark." He smiles. The menace is gone, and his other personality speaks. "If the burn is unreachable by truck, they drop my crew. We hike miles in with hundred-pound packs on our backs. We kill that fire and haul those packs out. If she sparks up again and headquarters has to send someone else after us to mop up, we've failed." Mox backhands my chest. "We don't fail." He reaches for the door. "Come meet the guys."

Back in the lobby, there are high fives and back-slaps, and I can't believe these are the same men who stared me down when I arrived. They don't speak much.

They don't respond to verbal greetings. But if they're pissed I'm here, they hide it well.

Two of them are a matched set, leaning short and built like bulldozers. Their gazes flit around the room. Jumpy fellas.

The other guy is different. Tall and massive and scarred. A sweep of thick blond hair on top and a goatee, and the only one of the four without a brown jacket. There's no jumpy in him. His gaze is soft and reaching.

"Fez, Fatty, Koss, may I present Jake King," Mox says. "Should he pass smoke-jumper recs, he'll be a probationary member of our crew. Now to the Jeep."

"Hold up. I need to tell a friend my news." I smile. "Then I have to reserve a room at the villa. So if you don't mind—"

"She'll wait. Let Salome wait." Mox walks up to me. "And my crew doesn't sweat small stuff. If you survive training, you'll live with us."

I stare at him. It's a command, and I bristle. I joined five minutes ago, and his invisible tentacles already try to wrap up every part of my life.

"I'm going to see her, now," I say. "If the apartment offer stands after that, I'll take it."

Fatty and Fez stop jostling in the doorway. Mox is unreadable.

"Let him go, Mox." Koss, the watcher, slaps my back and stares into me. "It's not every day you join a hotshot rappelling crew."

Mox nods, grins. "It was just a suggestion, kid." He reaches into his pocket and tosses me an apartment key. "Three Vista Estates. See you in a few months. Maybe." His face darkens, and his voice lowers. "Take my advice. Come on, guys." Mox shoves Fatty and Fez out of the building.

Koss doesn't move. He looks down, then raises his gaze. "Do you trust your friend?" He speaks so low, I'm not certain he spoke.

"Salome?" I ask.

He doesn't twitch.

"With my life."

"Then visit her often. It's those guys who have nobody on the outside . . . they can't stand up against it."

I shrug and nod.

He nods back. "Scottie is a good man. No matter what you hear—he isn't a rat, and he didn't bail."

"Koss!" Mox's head pokes through the door. "You coming?"

Koss slowly turns. "Talking training with the new guy." He looks over his shoulder. "Those suggestions help?"

"Yeah," I say. "Appreciate it."

Koss steps out and leaves me alone. I swallow hard.

It. What it *am I supposed to stand against?*

I peek out the door. Mox leans over the front bar of his Jeep. His hand flexes and tightens. I do the same with mine.

Let's get this started.

CHAPTER 13

APRIL COMES IN HOT and lonely.

Inside, I'm cold. There are too many things about Salome I don't understand. Why she can't see the difference between her brother and me, why she stopped coming over, why she couldn't bear to say good-bye. It's just stupid. And she's not stupid.

I roll onto my back and stare at the coils on the bunk above mine. It's my first visit to Herndon, and one night in, I already hate it.

I roll over and stare out at sleeping giants. The Cascade Foothills and the Trinity Alps surround.

"Everybody up." A dark silhouette fills the doorway.

"My name is Clancy. My job is to get you in shape. Whether you end up suited for aerial delivery, Type I hand-crew work, or ecosystem management, you all must be prepared for isolated-wildland fire suppression. Which means you will go through me."

I scratch my head. "Isn't this firefighter training?"

He walks toward me, leans over, and stares. "All of you except for one know the rigors of fighting wildfire. But none of you has any idea what it's like to hurtle out of a DC-3, twisting and free-falling into hell on earth. To watch your chute deploy, to land butt up in a one-hundred-fifty-foot ponderosa. To let down into charred field, run top speed five miles into the teeth of a blaze with near a hundred pounds on your back.

"Up!"

I jump up, my body quivering with the thought. "What are we doing standing here?" I spin a circle and watch twenty men groan and shake their heads. "What's first?"

Clancy chuckles, then laughs, and slowly others join in. "So green. Let me take a look at the young King." He stares hard, but his eyes gleam. "So far you live up to your reputation. Everyone, meet me outside in five minutes for a light run."

I'm outside in two, stretching and jumping and

watching men who want nothing to do with me spill out of our quarters. They gather in a circle, twenty paces from where I sit and stretch. Clancy plops down beside me.

"You don't deserve to be here. The other men aren't gonna like you." Clancy stares straight ahead.

"I'm used to that."

"I'm supposed to be hard on you."

"I'm used to that, too."

Clancy smiles. "These guys are veterans. They know what a run through the woods is like. That in mind, you want to lead? The path is clearly marked. Five miles. If you run out of gas, well, I'm sure they'd all appreciate a leisurely pace on Day One."

"Yeah!"

We walk to the trailhead.

"Jake here has offered to take point." Clancy shouts. "Keep your feet up. Go, Jake."

I leap into the woods, weave around trees, and skip over fallen branches. Behind me there is a smattering of voices, then all falls silent but my breath and the crackling of the twigs.

Faster.

A crunch behind me. I glance over my shoulder. It's Clancy. Gaining. I quicken my pace, he quickens his, and when I reach the end of the loop, he's only ten paces back.

I break back into the clearing, bounce, and stretch. "Can we go again?"

Clancy stumbles around, his mouth hanging open, hands clasped firmly on top of his head. He glances at the stopwatch.

"Twenty-five minutes." He gulps air. "That was twenty-five minutes."

"I'm sorry," I say. "I'll go faster."

He tries to laugh, grabs his waist, and winces. "You will never lead again."

MY FIRST WEEKS PASS, and I'm in heaven. We learn parachute landings and airplane exits and letdowns from eighty-foot pine giants. Then we add the gear. Sixty pounds of weight accompany us on our runs. It will not slow me down. I lap most of the group on seven-mile full-pack runs. Twice, I win.

I love it, love it all. The tree-climbing, the firefighting techniques, safety school . . . but Clancy wakes us on a beautiful Monday with the best news of all. "We're going up."

This will be a clear-sky jump onto a wide-open field.

We clamor into the plane, spiral higher, and pull the door. The engine roars, the draft licks my hands, and even from this height the air smells of sweet pine.

I turn into the plane. Our load is six. Four peaked faces, Grandier—a French guy not too much older than me—and myself.

Hankinson, our jump instructor, runs it all our first time out. He whips draft streamers out the open door, watches them flutter in red and blue, and yells toward the pilot.

"It's good."

We cruise to 2,700 feet, and my heart pulses. I'm here. Completely. I'm alive. Completely. How I got here docs not matter. Dad's calls and my lack of experience fade away. Heaven has reached down, and for this instant, I'm a believer.

Hankinson slaps my back, screams in my ear. "Little draft. It's all you, Jake. To the door."

The world whips by, yanks at me, tugs at my heart.

"Jump!"

I leap forward. All senses fire, and I free-fall.

"Jump one thousand, look one thousand, reach one thousand . . ."

I stabilize and hurtle like a bullet for the ground. I reach for the pull cord, force my hand loose.

"Wait one thousand, pull one thous—!"

My torso thrusts back, and the red chute unfurls against the blue sky.

"Whoa!"

I glance toward the ground. I'm too far left. I yank the toggle and float gently into the field. I hit soft, roll, and stand as the chute collapses over me.

I fight out, raise my arms, and scream.

"Again! Yeah. Do it again!"

This is my life. My time.

The following weeks, we practice leaping into terrain, collapsing into trees. We learn to use the tools and chainsaw trees and set back fires. There is nothing better than this job and the rush it brings.

Then training ends.

I feel lost. Here in Herndon I've found what I've been looking for. Why rappel from a copter when you could leap from an airplane?

But it's not right either. Salome's laugh isn't here. And while she finished senior year, graduated, shared that laugh with her friends, I've almost forgotten what it sounds like.

On our last day, I wake early and wander to the tarmac. I run my hands over the planes, now my friends, that carried me to thrill after thrill.

"I'm sorry I wasn't able to push you." Clancy stands at my side. "But you pushed yourself plenty." He looks at me, and I drop my gaze. "I finished my report. I ranked you as high as they come. Should be enough for Richardson."

I nod and stare off.

"That is what you wanted, isn't that right, son?"

"I guess so."

"Mox is as good a fighter as I've ever known. You'll learn a ton about rappelling." He breathes deep. "But when you're done in Brockton, after you get your years in, you come back. There's a place for you here. You're one heck of a kid."

I force a smile. *Then why won't she return my texts?*

CHAPTER 14

MY NEW HOME RESTS JUST outside of town and overlooks the Apido Valley. Apart from a few Immortals, it's quiet and ghostlike during winter, but now that summer's here, Vista Estates bustles with crazies and do-gooders all here to do one thing: knock the crap out of wildfires.

It's a rowdy bunch, more than half born-and-bred Brockton boys. Kyle had lived here. Had Scottie stuck around, it would have been his home, too.

I haul my stuff to number three. Mox's crew is housed nearest the helicopters and apart from the fifty other full- and part-timers. Judging from the AC/DC that blares out his open window, it's likely those others don't mind.

"Will you look at that?"

I glance over my shoulder and set down my duffel.

Will and the rest of Bulldozer Crew #1 walk up to me. "You better just be visiting."

Chuckles change to stone-faced seriousness.

I shake my head. "Mox picked me up."

The thin, balding fighter on the right—the one with Scottie's expressions—tenses. "The Forest Service *has* turned into a Forest Circus. You have no fire experience except backyard barbecues, and you're on a rappel team?"

"He's got a daddy. Ain't that right?" This speaker is new to Brockton, but he's already up on the situation. "A daddy with Richardson's ear."

I want to tell them that I didn't ask for Dad's help. That if a certain friend of mine would study journalism in Anchorage, I'd have no quarrel smoke-jumping in Alaska. What they say is true—I don't belong here. I know Dad worked the phone, and Mox hates that I came.

"Leave him alone." Will steps up and shakes my hand. "If there's better proof of Moxie's character, I've not heard it." Will throws his arms around his two buddies. "And after the toll the King family has taken on him. What was your brother thinking? Mox is a saint of a man, I'd say."

I shrug. "I don't keep track of what Scottie does, but I've never heard him lie. Ever."

Will lowers his arms and points at the open window. "He caused a great man pain. Mox has lost a lot of young men to stupidity. He deserves better than the investigation your brother put him, and all of us, through." His gaze turns to me. "Make it up to him. Listen and do what he says. Come on, guys."

They jostle on and leave me alone on the step.

I breathe deep. *Scottie caused pain? That's my job.* The proof was scarred into Kyle's face. This crew is my last chance to make things right.

I dig out my key and push through the door. Koss sits at the kitchen table and greets me with a smile.

"You're rooming with me. If you don't mind."

"That's fine." I dump my backpack and duffel in the entry and look around.

The walls are green, least I think that's the base color. Paint-ball explosions splotch every surface, every lamp and couch. Koss stands, chuckles, and glances around. His welted, reddened cheeks stretch into a grin. "It was a good fight."

I puff out air. "You guys have rules?"

"Yeah." He stretches, and muscles ripple beneath his white T-shirt. "No goggles allowed, and no shots below the neck."

I love it here. I'm home.

"The others went for a swim to wash off. I waited for you." He exhales hard and checks his watch. "Up for a hike?"

I nod and throw on my boots.

We descend into Apido Canyon. The only way down is a long, winding trail hemmed in with pine spires that stretch back toward the villa. Koss leads. I don't know what he wants to say, but he's in no hurry to speak.

"So how many years you been with the Forest Service?" I ask.

"Fifteen in California."

More silence. I roll my eyes and try again.

"You been on Mox's crew the whole time?"

Koss nods.

Strange, I haven't seen him around. Brockton isn't that big. A guy this imposing would be easy to spot. I tell him as much.

"I don't spend too much time here. My fiancée lives in Holdingford. We'll marry in December."

"Well, congrats. What's her name?"

Koss bends down and picks up a branch, and I stop short. He stares at his stick, his voice now far off. "No names. Keep their names to yourself."

"Whose?" I shift my feet and try to catch Koss's gaze. When he does look up, his eyes are sad, and I wish he'd go back to his twig.

His reaches out and squeezes my shoulder. "You're so young." Koss stares back up the trail. "What's said here, stays here. Can I trust you on that?"

"Yeah, I think so."

Koss looks at me hard, chuckles. "You're the second King son I've spoken to about this. The first one listened to me."

"Scottie."

"I will make it brief. Mox is going to give you something to wear. It'll feel good. It'll feel like you're part of something. You might even feel like you owe him something. After you get comfortable in it, he'll ask you to join his little band. You say no to both offers."

My face must look blank because he rolls his eyes and tightens his jaw. "He'll offer you a brown Immortals jacket. If you take it, you'll be one of them—an Immortal. And that would be just fine if it stopped there, but being one comes with a price, and when there's an opening, he'll ask you to join his club. Let's call it the Rush Club. Don't do it. Scottie listened and walked out of here."

"I'm different than Scottie."

"I know."

"That's it? That's the reason for all this secrecy?"

"That's all."

"Those jackets, I've been wondering about them a long time. If you can give me a good reason not to take one, fine. But otherwise . . ."

Koss bends down, takes that twig he holds, and scratches in the dirt. Draws first a circle, then an arrow, like a one-handed clock. He straightens.

"Sometimes it's best to trust. I need you to trust me." He looks down, points at the drawing. "When we started this, I thought we were doing right. Two crazy rookies passing time and taking matters into our own hands." He stares at me. "But since I left the club—well, it's gotten out of hand. Good kids dying in the spin."

In the spin. In the spin. Kyle!

"Kyle said that. He said he was 'in the spin.'" I point at Koss. "Do you know what happened to Kyle?"

Koss inhales, taps the ground with his stick. "*That* happened to Kyle. Same as what happens to them all. Sooner or later the spin catches you. Look, Mox doesn't want you. He's probably going to push you extra hard.

And now that he's mad at your brother?" He sighs. "Jake, you stay with me, and you'll be okay. Thing is, eventually he'll get you alone. Then you say no to his offers." He grinds his toe across the ground, erasing the clock face. "Or you could do the next best thing. Quit and leave town now."

I shake my head. "You're kidding, right?"

He says nothing. Koss pulls a cigarette from behind his ear and works it hard.

"People have been down on me my whole life, and I'm still here." I point down to the dirt. "Whatever that thing was you warned me about, if it has anything to do with getting a jacket, I'm taking it. To be on a rappel crew and to join a bunch of adrenaline junkies like the Immortals—this is like a dream. I'll take care of me."

"You talk about what you don't know." His voice lowers to a whisper. "Don't tell me about the Immortals. Don't lecture me with rumor. The Rush Club was *my* idea. Young, stupid me." He swallows, rubs his eyes hard. "But I didn't make the rules. You got to believe me, I didn't make the rules. That was all Mox."

Koss grabs my shoulders, and his eyes plead. His hands are vises. There are precious few times I've felt I couldn't break free, but I know I'm stuck here until he lets me go.

"Since I don't know what you're talking about, I forgive you. Can you let me go?"

"Yeah." He releases me. "I'll let you go."

The next minute fills with awkward silence.

Koss straightens. "So you're sticking around?"

"I'm not Scottie." I step back and massage my arms. "Tell me about Kyle. He was an Immortal. Where did he get his jack—"

"Not another word." Koss purses his lips. "We never spoke. My job's done."

He lights up again, and we walk back up the trail. He talks easily now. We cover his nameless fiancée, his home in Montana, and life on the fire line. Our earlier conversation becomes a weird, irregular heartbeat that doesn't fit with the rest of the day's easy rhythm.

I unpack, settle onto the colorful couch, and the three swimmers reappear dead drunk. Fez and Fatty fall into the place, and Mox stumbles over them, regains his balance. I stand to greet, but two men stay down, passed out on the floor. Mox looks at me, and it's a horrible gaze. Because he's still in control of it. His body's loaded and barely vertical, but somehow his eyes still pierce. Terrifying.

"Come on, Jake. Give me a hand." Koss walks to Fatty, hoists him up as if he was hollow. I reach down and muscle Fez over my shoulder. I follow Koss into the second bedroom and dump Fez into his bunk.

I collapse into my own bed and wonder how it is Dad knows so little. This is everything he hates. The wildness, the irresponsibility. This isn't the norm for firefighter crews. He lobbied me onto an aberration, an outlier, the one crew in California as crazy and reckless as the fires we'll face.

TRAINING IN BROCHTON IS a breeze. Two weeks of conditioning followed by rappelling and helicopter work. After leaping from planes, sliding down a cable hanging from a copter feels natural.

We gather in the old hangar turned gymnasium for refresher training and physical checks. Fats and Fez shove and joke and wait for their chance to impress.

"Wilson, Fatty."

Fatty rises to catcalls and whistles, struts slowly up to the front of the gym. He turns, lifts up his T-shirt, and flexes his biceps.

"You all want some of me?" He laughs, and the firemen assembled hoot.

I cringe. It's a gruesome thing to see.

He fails every test. Sit-ups. Push-ups. Fails them all. But they wink and nod him by.

He flops back down beside me. "There's more lee-way here than in Herndon." He pats his gut after his two-pull-up effort. "As long as I make weight, I'll be fine." Fatty slaps my back and gazes around the gym.

"King, Jake."

I stand when called. Around me it's silent. I approach the pull-up bar and peel off forty-six in a minute. I walk through the stares and plop back down by Fatty.

"Sheesh. You're like some monkey boy."

I smile and gaze across the room at Mox and Koss. They lean against the wall, watching. Koss grins back, but Mox's eyes are slits.

After our recs are complete, our crew walks from the gym back to the villa.

"What you been eating?" Fez grabs my biceps, and I pull away. "No Twinkies. That's for sure."

Mox leads the pack. Koss joins him, reaches out, and grabs him by the scruff of the neck. "Kid might turn out just fine."

"A few push-ups—"

"Forty-one in a minute. One-armed?" Fatty chimes in.

"And rabbits can run—"

"That was a base record." Fez nods in my direction.

"Doesn't mean anything when trees fall and wind shifts. Doesn't mean anything when the kid's fire experience is a birthday candle. When his dad and Richardson force him on—"

Koss steps in front of Mox. "Let it go. It's done."

Mox peeks back at me, then forward to Koss. "No, my friend. It's just beginning."

CHAPTER 15

MONTHS PASS, AND WILDFIRE season begins.

My first drops are uneventful. Small fires easily extinguished. But with each rappel, I see the skill of my crewmates. We zip 250 feet straight down from the copter on a half-inch rope in fifteen seconds. Then comes their genius, their art. Mox and Koss hit the ground, circle, and their eyes meet. They speak without words, and both know it all—safety zones, wind shifts, urgency— they close their eyes for a moment, and when they open them, everything is clear, the deadly dance begins, and in hours the fire will surrender.

Koss slowly brings me into the blaze, teaches me the

tells of each fire. But not Mox. He barks at me with the hate of the burn. Then I watch him throw himself in front of the fiery beast, all to save a house. An empty house. And I have no idea what to think of him anymore.

Koss no longer warns me about the club, and I don't want him to. Life with the guys feels so good. Rappelling into fires by day, partying extreme-style all night. Then the villa fills with faces I've never before seen in Brockton. It's as if there's a secret entrance to town I never knew about. Koss watches the mayhem, then quickly vanishes into our room.

I slap on a smile, try to find a friendly face in the crowd. For a while it works. The craziness rubs off, and I feel part of this crew. Then a different face worms into my mind. I haven't heard from Salome in months; it's the longest we've ever been apart.

Soon I lie on my bed and listen to Koss snore and wonder what she's doing now.

IN THE MORNING, THE FLOOR is littered with beer cans. Mox, Fatty, and Fez are gone, vanished along with the other Immortals who wander the estates. So far, I've seen eighteen different Immortals jackets. On the rappel crew, the hand crew, the dozer crew. When here, they strut around the condo like they're holding some inside joke.

That's fine by me, because there's always Koss. He's the older brother Scottie never was, the one I never knew I wanted.

But hanging with Koss can't fill the big loss in this bargain.

I need to see her.

Three hours later I search the parking lots of Mid-Cal State. Her car has to be here. If I know her, and I do, she'll be studying.

The library.

Sure enough, her green Saab is nearest the door. Though it's Friday, I bet she'll be here all day.

I park and hop out, run my hand over the hood of the Saab. It's her. It's me.

Us.

I've been in this car a hundred times. We went everywhere together. Suddenly, my teeth chatter. Not because I'm cold, but because it's been so long. Months. Everything she wanted to be, she is. Everything she wanted me not to be, I've become.

I try the doors, and the passenger door gives. I slip inside and smell her. Filling my lungs with her should satisfy, but now I'm empty. My next jump, the zip into the forest, won't be enough either. The rappel is not enough, not without . . .

I peek out at the library.

Salome. She stands and leans against a tree, hugging her books. The perfect university brochure shot. She smiles and talks to friends I don't know.

I grab a pencil from the glove compartment and scribble a note.

It's me. Jake.

Been too long. Got things to say. I see you're busy right now. Tomorrow? 7:00? I'll be right here. Call my cell.

Miss you, friend.

I stare at my note, shake my head, and erase the last word.

Miss you.

I look around the car, see her light green jacket, and grab it.

The note needs one more line.

In case you're thinking of saying no, took jacket as ransom.

I lay the note on her dash and slip away before she sees me. Halfway home, my cell rings.

"Hey," I say.

There's a pause on the other end.

"I'll be waiting."

Click.

* * *

"WHERE HAVE YOU BEEN, Jake?" Mox demands when I get home.

I step into our apartment, where Fez, Fatty, and Mox are working out, and gently lay Salome's jacket on the table. "I needed to get away."

Mox hops off the stationary bike, stares at the jacket. "I bet." He smirks. "Salome took you looking like that?"

"Shut up. She's none of your business."

Fatty drops from the pull-up bar, and Fez pauses mid-push-up.

"Watch your words, Jake. You may be a freakish physical specimen, but you're still a kid who Moxie's been more than generous with." Fez slams out ten more and stands. "Mox is your lead. Even here." He and Mox shoot glances at each other.

Mox licks his lips, breaks into a smile, and the room relaxes. "I know, kid. You and Salome are best friends." He walks nearer. "Richardson called. We're off the rotation. Seems somebody is still talking about Kyle's death. Seems my name keeps coming up, and I'm in for more questions. Been talking to anyone lately, Jake?"

"Off the rotation? No drops?" I curse, knowing how much I needed that rush. "No, I haven't talked to anyone." I flop onto the couch, darkness filling my mind, and let my head swivel toward Mox. "I don't know anything about it. You haven't told me about any of the guys that died. So, Mox, how often is this going to happen?"

That same tense feeling grips the room. It's always like that. Only Koss can question Mox, or the team freaks.

Mox climbs back onto the bicycle. I watch his hands—his tell. He's crap at poker because he can't control them. Knuckles whiten on the handlebars, but the words are silk. "We'll have to find diversions to keep us sharp. Tomorrow night we should—"

"Got plans," I say. "I won't be joining you guys."

"Were you invited?" Mox asks.

"No. I wasn't. Isn't that right, Fatty?"

He peeks at Mox and hangs silent from the bar.

"While we're on the subject, why isn't Koss invited on your rampages? I don't imagine *his* dad got him on your crew." I rise, step up to the cycle, and stare at Mox. He stares back.

Silence.

"Is everybody here mute?"

I've never seen these guys flustered, but here they are red-cheeked. Mox crosses his arms. "You done, Jake?"

"I've got so many questions." I turn from him and see Fez and Fatty sneaking toward the back room. "Where are you two going?" They slowly turn. "Don't have the right words? Mox, tell them what to say. Then they can join the conversation."

"*You done*, Jake?"

Seeing Salome has opened a floodgate that I don't know how to close, and I push on. "Why doesn't Koss wear a jacket? And why haven't you given me one? There must be a closet filled with them around here somewhere. But my biggest question: What happened to Kyle . . . and to Drew?"

Mox flies off the bike and grabs me by my coat. He rears back, and I brace.

"I'm only asking questions. This is my crew—we've been fighting fire together for more than a month. Don't I have a right to know anything?" I look at him, try to copy the cool look Salome gives, and shake my head.

He shoves me back and turns away from me.

Emotions I can't figure out surge through me. "Like it or not, I'm here. And I'm staying."

My gaze sharpens, scans. In the corner, cans of spray paint lie in a heap.

"And another question, while I have your attention." I walk over, grab one, shake hard, and spray. Round and round, I darken a huge red circle on the wall. One quick stroke for the arrow finishes it off. "What is this thing?"

Frozen. Three strong firefighters turn white and

stare at the clocklike thing, at bloodred paint that drips toward the carpet.

"Where'd he see it?" Fatty whispers.

"Koss." Fez folds his arms. "I told you, Mox. It was bound to happen."

"Don't be a fool. Koss didn't say anything. Only one possibility." Mox walks up to the wall, runs his finger through the red paint. "What do you know about this?"

"Nothing," I say. "I know nothing about any of you."

A cloud passes in front of the sun, and the room darkens. We stare at each other in the shadow.

Mox looks over his shoulder. "Get out of here, Jake. Pack your things and get out."

I run my hand through my hair. "What do you mean? Can you do that?"

"I can do anything I want. Now go!"

"Doesn't Richardson, um . . ." I peek at Fatty. He looks as confused as I am.

"Okay," I say, "I'm a—I'm getting my things." I split Fez and Fatty, enter my bedroom, and jam all I own into my backpack. Without Koss here, I don't know what's real and what's not. I do know that in the main room, voices rise.

"But even you can't dump a crewmate. It doesn't matter—"

Crash. Glass shatters on the other side of the wall.

I swallow hard and hurry out to the table for Salome's jacket. It's gone. Another rests in its place. My jacket. Jake, with an *I* emblazoned on the back.

My fingers reach out to stroke it. The hum of the lights, the buzz from the old refrigerator, the fly buzzing around my head—each noise strengthens. My jacket. My chance. My hand clenches around the sleeve.

"Stay," Mox says. "You just earned that."

Don't take the jacket.

I release it and turn to face them.

"You told me to leave."

Mox clenches his jaw and glances at Fez, who gives an exaggerated nod.

When Mox looks back to me, he stares at my shoes. "I can't fire anybody. I found that out early on. Call that a test. Being an Immortal takes loyalty, obedience, and strength. I'm not used to being handled like that, kid. You belong. You're one of us."

"I've never seen anyone do that to Mox. Have you, Fats?" Fez exhales hard.

"Nope. Not and live to tell about it." He winks and turns to me. "Join us."

"I thought I already had." Behind me, my fingers keep walking over the jacket. It feels really good.

"Yes and no." Mox exhales hard and throws his arm around my neck. "We want you to be a part of more than the crew. We've got something to show you this week." I see Salome's jacket in Mox's hands. He fiddles, strokes. It's not right.

"Give me her jacket."

"That's the thing. You can't wear both." He looks toward the ceiling.

The cloud descends on my head again.

A dark streak flashes across Mox's face and vanishes. "She'll understand. She always understands, doesn't she?"

I nod and stare at my jacket, at my name on it. I've never been part of anything.

Don't take the jacket.

Salome and me, we're different now. Maybe more, maybe less. For sure different. I don't know what she'll understand.

I look at the wall I just painted.

I know they're playing me, sucking me in. I can feel it.

"What is that round clock thing? Will you at least tell me that?"

Mox joins me. "I'll do better than that, kid. Join the Immortals, and when the time is right, I'll show you."

The Immortals fit. I can't deny it. I pick up the jacket and slide it on.

Mox nods and smiles. "Good. We're heading to the caves tomorrow. You in?"

I look at Fatty. He smiles and nods back.

Loyalty. Obedience.

"You're inviting me? Yeah. I'm in."

Mox turns toward his room. "I feel bad about this jacket. I'll wash it for her." He presses it against his face, like a dog getting a scent. "Pretty girl."

CHAPTER 16

I SPEND THE NEXT MORNING pacing my
room, fog filling my mind. Thought of the jacket always
whooshed the mind clear, but now, wearing my own,
nothing makes sense. The thought of the caves is a drug,
an upper that promises to clear my head, but Salome's a
drug, too. A tranquilizer with an exciting kick.

I step into the afternoon. Koss alone sits in the room.
He stares at the jacket I wear, at the wall I painted.

"Did you tell them where you saw that?"

"No."

"And then, let me guess, Mox blew."

"Sort of."

Koss walks toward me, stares down at me. "Suddenly, Mox is a different man. Was I right? He invited you to join the Immortals and offered you this spiffy jacket . . ." He backhands my chest. ". . . and all is wonderful."

I frown and nod.

"Well, well. One smart King and one dumb one." He turns to leave.

"Koss. Please." I swallow hard. "Ever since I was little, I've seen these." I rub my sleeves. "And ever since I was little, it's been black up here." I point at my head. "And one makes the other clear."

"Are you clear now?"

"No."

"You got what you wanted and found it wasn't what you needed, and you're blowing it with the only one who can save you."

He stops but does not turn. His head droops. "I don't know how to watch over you, kid. Not when you don't listen. There's more at work here than you know." He spins and stares. "Give it back. Today. Give it back."

Koss storms out.

I rub hands through my hair, collapse into the recliner, and whisper, "You don't know what it's like in here."

***

THE CUCHOO CLOCH IN the apartment clucks three times. Mox throws open his door. "Time to go, gentlemen. I have another meeting with Richardson at six thirty."

I nod. We'll be back in time for my talk with Salome. We reach for our jackets. I feel the weight of leather on my shoulders and stretch out my arms. It fits perfectly.

Mox smirks. "Ever cave-dived, Jake?"

"No."

"Claustrophobic?"

"No."

"Onward."

We pile into Mox's jeep. I sit in back behind the bar. It feels right . . . for two minutes. We drive for an hour. I think of Salome the whole time. I see her face and hear her words and feel like an asshole. If I don't make it back in time . . . How often have I let her down? I slump and fold my arms. I've no idea where we are.

We squeal to a stop, and everyone moves at double time. I crawl out and stretch.

"Let's do the Pinch." Fez hops out.

Mox rubs his stubble and squints. "It's Jake's first time."

"He's up to it." Fez looks at me as if it was a question.

The guys unload gear—miner's helmets glowing with

carbide flames, one tank of oxygen, and flippers. They laugh and strip to T-shirts and shorts.

"When do I get to know what we're doing?" I ask.

"Just a stroll through a cave," Mox says, and tosses me his jacket. "New guy carries the tank."

I lay his coat in the Jeep. "Why do we need a tank on a stroll?"

Nobody answers, and I strip quick and fall in line behind the other three. We set off down a brush-covered hill dotted with giant rock formations. They speed to a trot, and I let them go, lean against a vertical rock face.

Late. I'm going to be way late. Sorry, Salome. I set down the oxygen and the miner's helmet.

From ahead, Mox hollers, "Where's the air?" His outline appears, stiff and angry. He marches toward me, reaches down for the tank, turns, and disappears.

I shuffle after him. I'll see Salome tonight and patch it all up. Late is better than not at all.

Ahead, Mox fills the afternoon with curses.

Fatty calls, "We're here."

CHAPTER 17

THE OPENING TO THE CAVE resembles a mouth with two teeth jagging up from the earth. The guys throw on their gear, squeeze into helmets. Three blue lights turn to me, and I squint, shielding my eyes with my arm.

"Aren't you coming?" The light with Fez's voice steps nearer.

I pause. "Show me how to light up the carbide."

"No, kid," Mox says. "Everyone's on his own. Grab the tank, Fatty."

They turn and walk toward the opening. Five feet around, the crack in a boulder mound leads straight into the side of a hill. I listen to their footsteps. That mouth swallows all sound.

I cup my hands and call, "What do you want me to do?"

"Don't care," Mox says. "Go whine in the Jeep. No use standing there."

They disappear. His voice is already faint. "We won't be coming out on this side."

I stare at the hole. It stares back at me. They found Kyle floating in a cave nearby. I wonder where. I wonder if here. My heartbeat flutters.

Best keep close to 'em. I jog back to my helmet and strap it on. I fight with the helmet lamp, but can't get it to flame and race back toward the cave mouth. I bend down, catch a flash of light in the distance.

I step in and make for the spot. It could be them, but it might just be the direction they're looking. It's all I've got.

"Hold up. I'm coming!"

No reply. I step forward and bats swarm around my head. "Mox?"

Muffled laughter up ahead, and I grope forward in darkness. I'm descending. Loose rock gives way beneath my hiking shoes, and I slide down five feet, maybe ten. All is cold and black, and I turn. The entrance is gone. So is my hand, inches in front of my face.

I face front and strain to hear any noise. Beneath the squeak of dive-bombing bats, there's a new sound, a gurgling. Water.

I bend and move toward it—one hand on the ceiling, one on the wall. The sides of the cave pinch in until they scrape my arms. I try to step back, uphill. My shoulders wedge, and for a moment I'm trapped beneath the earth.

Blood pounds in my ears. I stick out my leg and wave it back and forth. It feels like the Pinch opens. I take a deep breath and force my body forward. The earth releases me, and I stumble on, tumble ten feet off an outcropping, and land with a splash. Water races over me, and steals my breath. I stand and gasp in the subterranean stream.

Mox's laugh. Loud and clear, just ahead. I splash wildly through the stream—the water laps my thighs, deepens.

"I'm right here! Mox!"

Ahead I hear the jumping of some tremendous fish. Water swirls around my waist, and I pause. I'm cold. My feet are losing feeling. I need to get out of here fast.

I wade forward, hands out to the sides. One strikes metal. The tank. It swirls around and around.

Something's not right. Where are they? I inch ahead and tap riverbed rock with my foot. Another giant step. I bounce on my front toe and try to bear weight. My foot must be numb. I feel nothing.

Solid footing gives way, and I plunge beneath the waterline. My hands fly out, brace against the smooth rock on all sides.

The tube that surrounds me is so tight there's no use kicking. I wriggle my arms above my head, and my hands slip off the stone.

My mind clears.

I hurdle downward, deeper into my tomb. I have thirty seconds of air. Down, down. Then *whoosh*, I enter another fast-flowing river that sweeps me ahead into darkness. My helmet bounces off rocky outcroppings; my flesh rips off stone daggers.

Pain sizzles over my shoulders, but it doesn't hurt for long. I'm too busy dying.

I've a few seconds of air left, and I swim with the current, explode upward. My head pops out of water and I gasp, whisk out beneath a starry sky. The river bubbles, and I fight my way to the edge, haul up onto my belly.

"Oh. Oh." The word fights out in jagged whispers.

My heartbeat slows, then quickens. I recognize the huge rock in front of me and realize I'm a long way from the Jeep.

I stagger up, bleed, and the earth spins. I stumble forward and hear Koss's voice. *Stay away from Mox. Say no to his offers. He hates you.* I glance off a tree and run faster. Time blurs. My vision blurs. I break out of trees and see the empty Jeep.

I crash into the back, collapse into the seat, and throw up.

My world shakes, I shake, and my thoughts can't stay still.

I reach for a jacket, huddle beneath, and wait to die. I slip into a dream, a beautiful one. Scottie and I talk with sleepy voices, tucked in sleeping bags beside a roaring fire. Through the smoke, I see Mom and Dad, huddled together, their voices soft and warm. The world is right. Everything's right.

Until Scottie stands and yanks my sleeping bag and the chill reaches bone.

I try to holler, but I get colder and colder, and my voice freezes in my throat.

My body jerks hard, and I hear muddled voices. "He's still alive."

"He got through without air. Moxie, let it go."

"WELCOME BACK."

A gentle hand plays with my hair, and I crack an eyelid. It's dark, but it's warm in my room, and Salome sits on the bed.

I exhale slowly. "I'm glad it's you—Wait, you shouldn't be here." I wring my hands beneath the sheets. Skin burns. A cold burn.

"Is that a way to greet a friend? I could probably beat you to a pulp right now."

I close my eyes. I can't put it together—why Salome is in the villa she hates, how I got here in the first place. I only know I'm a fool, and if I had the choice over again, I wouldn't have gone in that cave.

A shiver works my body, and Salome tucks blankets over my shoulders.

"How—"

"Shut up." She smiles. "I'll tell you the whole bizarre story, or the majority of it, including the headline— 'Keeping Guarantees Important to Young Women.'" She looks away.

She continues. "I found your note and sat in the car for half an hour. I read that note over and over. I called three friends and my mom before I called you. Do you know what she said? Absolutely nothing." Salome sighs. "I have a great mom."

"Yeah, you do. And I'm sorry—"

She places her hand on my mouth and shakes her head. "So I headed back home and crawled into bed, with visions of you in my head. I've been trying hard to get rid of those. Then the phone rang."

"For you?"

She doesn't answer. "It was a nice guy, and he wanted to stop by Saturday."

My jaw tightens. "You said no."

"I said, 'I already have plans.'"

Salome places her hands on her lap, and stares at them. My face now burns hot.

"Who was the jerk?"

She gazes hard at me.

"Who called you?" I ask.

"What right do you have to know? He's a good guy."

I wince, and she continues. "So all day yesterday I wait for seven o'clock. Because someone I hadn't seen in way too long wanted to see me. And I wanted to see him. I waited until nine, went home, and called the other guy. I told him to come right over."

"You called—"

"Just shut up. Ten minutes later, I heard the knock.

And I'm dressed nice. I looked good. Because all day I'd been dreaming of having a good time, and I was going to have one. I threw on my happy face and threw open the door and just about threw up. Mox stood there dripping. He'd gotten my address from your emergency contact file. He was dazed and looked like he'd seen a ghost, which, now that I've seen you, wasn't too far from the truth. 'I need you,' he said."

My stomach lurches.

"'What you need,' I told him, 'is a slap in the face.' I started to lay into him about Drew, and he got a funny look. I'd say anxious, if he had an anxious bone in his body. He asked me to step outside. I told him to wait. I told him he came at a really bad time. But he grabbed my arm and yanked me to the road, and there you were, half dead in a Jeep."

"So I blew off conscious date number two, and hopped in back with the original unconscious note leaver. I assumed we were heading to the hospital, but no again, Mox the Magnificent insisted on bringing you here. Your friends, the fat one and the slimy one, carried you in and took off. They said they'd be back to check on us tomorrow, and tomorrow it is, and here you are."

"And here you are," I say.

She shakes her head. "How am I going to get rid of you?"

We sit in silence and look at each other. I wonder what she thinks. How many more times she'll put up with me.

"Your dad was here most of the night. He just left."

I nod.

"Bubbling Brooke stopped in, too. But she irritated your dad, and I think it may be some time before you see her again."

I roll my eyes. "I should've been at the library. I shouldn't have gone."

"When will you stop?" I whisper.

"Stop—"

"Coming for me?"

She turns. "I don't know. It's already different."

"'Cause I fight fire?"

"No. You're strong and brave, and I bet nobody on your crew can do what you do. I'm proud of that." She inhales. "But time goes by, and life changes, and I hoped that one day you'd join a crew somewhere far from this place. Where you could be you, and maybe I . . ."

She turns, and I follow her gaze to the balled-up brown jacket in the corner. She stands, walks over, and raises it to eye level.

"'Jake King,'" Salome reads. She drops it. Her gaze sticks to the floor. Minutes pass—they feel like hours—and she slowly returns to sit on the bed.

"Well, look at you. You put on their jacket. I guess it fits."

She rubs my forehead, but I know her—the gaze tells me she's not here.

"I know this makes no sense to you." I swallow hard. "But when I had no air, when I was sure I wasn't going to make it, I felt so . . . normal."

Salome closes her eyes. I can't watch. Again, she turns away. She can't watch me either.

CHAPTER 18

THERE IS A SUN. Strips of light cover me, and I look like a photonegative tiger. I stagger up from bed, wait for the room to still, and stumble to the shade to let the fireball in full.

Outside, Brockton cooks beneath the heat. It's the same town today as yesterday. The hardware store, Randall's filling station. It's the same place, hemmed in by mountains that womb and isolate us from the world.

But it's not. It's a different sun today shining on different mountains. The sun is brighter, the mountains not so protective, and the town, well, this morning it's just plain ignorant.

She's gone.

I RISE AND SHOWER. Water drips off blood-caked gashes on my arms and legs. I need to leave, to put as much space as possible between Mox and me. I dress with a grimace and step out into the heat. Minutes later, I wander Brockton's streets. I'm not much for thinking—it's uncomfortable to spend too much time in my head, and I walk blank-minded. I pass Dad's place, once my place. I stare at his neighbors'—once Salome's—home.

But the houses are quiet, and nothing draws me.

"You going to stand there in the street?"

Dad steps out the front door, squints in the sunlight, and clears his throat. I drop my jaw to speak, but nothing comes out.

Dad nods, walks slowly down the steps. "You well?"

"I—I don't know."

Dad strolls around front to Mom's garden. I should move toward him. I'm his son. But my feet grow heavy, and I've nothing to say.

"Ever think about your mom?"

"No," I lie.

"Will you sit with me?"

"I need to get back to—"

"Sit down, will you?"

I puff out air, walk onto the lawn, and plop beside him on the grass. It's silent.

Movement, in the corner of my eye. Dad rocks gently and stares straight ahead. I don't know the man who sits beside me.

"Well," I say. "This is great and all, but—"

Dad grabs my forearm and squeezes.

"You know how I felt when Scottie left. You can't imagine my thoughts when Mox came by and told me about your stunt. He went after you. He tried to stop you from your craziness and save you from yourself, but you did it anyway."

My arm hurts, and I pull away.

"I thought maybe a little discipline from a man like Moxie Stone would help." He rubs his face with both hands. "But I don't want to lose you, too.

"I'd have visited again, but they said you just needed rest." He slaps my back, and I wince. "You look good."

"I'm okay."

More silence. I peek at Dad, catch him peeking back.

"I want you to leave the Forest Service, Jake." His voice strengthens. "I know I pushed you into this. Your mom understood you; I never did. It seemed a decent fit." Dad turns back to the flowers. "What was this cave thing? That's where they found Kyle." Again, he clears his throat. "The pressure must be too much."

"You, Salome, Scottie, Koss, Mox. Every single one of you wants me off this crew. But none of you see what this crew does for me. They're wild and—"

"Think on it. I'll say no more." Dad stands, brushes off his jeans. "And if you ever want to, I mean, if you have time, maybe you'd want to visit." He gazes at the house. "It's pretty dark here without you guys." Dad reaches down and squeezes my shoulders. It burns, but I don't mind. "Take care of yourself, Jake."

My father disappears into the house.

I look down at my Immortals jacket. My *dad* wants me to quit?

I rise and take a right on Klaeburn. I need to get back to the villa, where there's no thinking needed. Fires burn, training takes over, knock them out. And the entire time my head is free and clear.

The rooms are empty.

I collapse on my bed, fall into restless sleep. Hours later, I wake. I stand and pull the shade. Mountains rise black on gray in the distance.

The cave debacle has faded, and the monster awakes. I need something, and I won't find it here.

I exit the villa. It's too quiet, and night sounds suddenly amplify. I start to jog and freeze. Up ahead, a gray shape vanishes down the path leading to the ravine. I scamper after it. The crunch of its feet stop, start, and stop again. The silhouette is either careful or paranoid, and I duck off the trail and into the woods.

I speed up and soon move beside it. It hates my being here and bends often to look into the trees, but I freeze and it's dark and soon it ignores me.

I let it go on ahead and follow twenty paces back. By the time I reach the bottom of the ravine I'm relaxed. Like I am with Salome—well, like I was.

I pause and circle in what once was a stream. Now it's dead—rocky and lifeless and cool in the night. I rub my arms as she had done, close my eyes, and see her sitting on my bed and wonder what makes this job so hard to leave.

Laughter. Lots of it. I light-foot forward through the darkness and wind through the ravine. I round a rocky outcropping and stop. A hundred feet ahead, a bonfire burns, and fiery tongues lick the sky. The flame sets near twenty faces glowing. I know them all.

I live with three.

They all wear their jackets, the one I have on my back. I slip behind my rocky shield and peek over the top.

"Well, gentlemen, we once again have an opening. We are nineteen. According to the rules, we must be twenty." Mox places his arm around Troy's shoulder. My buddy Troy. My left-him-laughing-in-front-of-Brooke's Troy.

My brown-jacketed Troy.

"Our new member has been appointed, and now only one item remains undone." He smiles. Fatty and Fez shuffle behind the fire, and I can't see a thing. They reappear, lugging a wooden disc ten feet in diameter. They lower it onto a stake and step back. The wood wobbles, steadies, and the men circle.

My breath catches, and I close my eyes. In my memory the images are clear—Koss scratches a clocklike drawing in the dirt, Mox wipes his finger in red spray paint. The wooden disc lifts, turns over in my mind, and both eyes shoot open.

They were never drawing a clock. It was this wheel.

"While you're in the spin, you will speak to nobody about your task. We won't speak to you." Mox sounds triumphant.

Troy looks at Mox. My buddy is scared. I see it one hundred feet away. "I do this, and I'm in?"

Mox says nothing.

"And then no more spins ever?" Troy looks around.

Nobody answers. He's staring down at this disc. I can't see all his face, but half is enough. Half says whatever's on the disc is more than he bargained for.

"Spin, spin." The chant starts slowly, quietly. It gathers steam. Eyes blaze, and the group bends down like they're worshipping this thing, like it holds the script of their lives. Only Troy still stands.

I want to call to him. I want to remind him he has a family and he doesn't have to do whatever this crackpot tells him. I want him to take off running my way. We'd outrun them. I know we could. I step out from behind the rock. Troy falls to his knees, grabs the disc, and gives it a whirl.

The chanting stops as the wheel turns and tilts and wobbles. It comes to a lazy rest, and everyone slowly stands.

Troy jogs over to Mox, grabs his sleeve. Troy tries to catch Mox's gaze but cannot. In the firelight, I see my friend's face blanch.

Mox rips his arm away and straightens his jacket.

"Welcome to the Rush Club."

CHAPTER 19

MY HEART RACES. It rarely races.

But an hour after the wheel was whisked away, after nineteen men snaked silently back toward the path that leads up to the villa, my heart pounds harder than ever. Because Troy still sits, head buried in his hands, in front of the embers of a fire.

I approach him quietly, and again feel the heavy press down on me. But this is a different heavy, a bad heavy, a weight that excites and sickens at the same time.

"Troy," I whisper. He doesn't move. "Troy?" He jerks around and stares at me with wide eyes. His gaze shifts to where the wheel was, where the stake still is, and crawls back to me.

"Just get here?"

"No."

My word acts like an electric jolt. He's on his feet. "What'd you see?"

I walk toward him, slap his back, and plop to the ground. "Not sure. I was hoping you could fill me in."

Troy eases down to the earth, and together we stare at flickering embers.

I lean into his shoulder. "Here's what I know. Nineteen guys, you'll make twenty. Guys from the dozer crew, the hand crews, and, of course, my sorry bunch minus Koss. Mox was in charge, as always. A big wheel came out. You spun, you freaked. 'Welcome to the Rush Club.'" I peek at Troy.

He nods. "You know, I always thought *you* were the freak. Even though we hung out, I'd go home and tell my folks you were crazy."

I dig in the dirt with my heel. "That's not so far off the truth."

"I mean, when I started seeing Cheyenne, she'd ask me why I'd want to hang with a guy who had a death wish. Remember your waterfall dive? What was that?"

I squeeze my forehead between thumb and forefinger. "People do strange things to feel normal."

His voice softens. "But at least you do your *own* thing. You don't let Mox or anybody get to you."

"Can't say that."

It's quiet for a long time.

Troy sighs. "I've done a lot of dumb things, especially when you're around."

I wave him off. "True."

A weighty silence falls. It's too big to lift. And in that silence a feeling births, a closeness with my friend that I've never felt. I know that whatever this club is, we're in it together. Fifteen minutes pass and we say nothing. In the distance, there's a howl, but we don't flinch. Because Troy is a friend. I'm not going anywhere.

We rise slowly and stomp out embers. It's dark, and I know Troy's dodging, so I grab him beneath the arm. "I need to know what I saw, and why you want something you think is cursed."

He sighs. "Can you see my face?"

"No," I say.

"I'm in the spin. The Rush Club has an opening, and I just need to get through initiation."

"Do what's on the wheel."

"Yeah," he whispers.

"Why'd they pick you?"

"They didn't. Immortals name their successor in case they don't . . ."

"Make it," I say.

Troy's fingers flex and loosen. "Carter named me."

"This club, you don't have to do this. Nobody can make you." I put my hand on his shoulder. "Think about this. You have a beautiful girl, and you don't *need* any of this. You're not like me."

"No"— his voice grows fainter—"but Mox can take away the circus. He trashes my reputation, and no rappel crew in the country will pull my cert again. And Cheyenne begged me to apply here. Close to family. It's the perfect place for us."

I nod, then frown. "But . . . you're not on a rappel crew."

He smiles weakly. "Mox said he was going to pick me up real soon. He said there'll be an opening, and this time he's going to be the one to fill it. That means we'll be on the same crew. Except I don't know how he's going to fit six rappellers in one copter."

He won't.

I lean over and rub my legs hard. "So does everyone join? Everyone just listens to Mox and half die?"

"No. There was this guy picked up by the hand crew earlier this year. Kyle's successor. He blew off Mox's offer of immortality."

My eyes widen.

"Yeah," he continues. "Rumor has it you know him pretty well."

CHAPTER 20

THE PATIO BEHIND OUR villa is quiet. Unusual for our crew. But I don't mind. Fatty tans on a burdened lounge chair and Fez chain-smokes over a crossword puzzle. That leaves Koss and me to work the grill.

"Good news." Mox saunters up to the barbecue, grabs a hot dog bare-fingered, and smokes it like a cigar. "We're back on rotation. Put the coals out. There's a fire up in Anderson."

Koss nods. Fez and Fatty whoop. And I take care of the coals.

Ten minutes later we get our orders, and we jog, geared up, onto the tarmac. We swing into the helicopter beneath the thumping of rotors. In the distance, a finger of black spirals into the sky.

This moment answers all the questions. The "why" Salome doesn't understand and the reason I'll never comply with Dad's request. Inside, I burn a joyful burn, and darkness flees. I hate fire. I want to kill it. But I love it. It dances in my mind.

We hover over the smoke. Radio scratches in the distance.

"Abort, guys. Wind shifts in the canyon." The copter pilot looks back and smiles. "It's turning ugly. Not your war today."

Nobody pays attention. We stare at Moxie's shadow. A red light flashes across his face.

We're near it. He smells it like I smell it. The mindless hate of an out-of-control burn. Only he smells it more. His hands slowly open, close. He gently rocks, trying to feel, starting to feel. Moxie's eyes gleam.

He reaches into a chest pocket, pulls out a picture, presses it against his chest, then quickly stuffs it back.

"Hover!" Mox steps out onto the helicopter's skids. "The IC has the call, and this IC says, yeehaw!" Mox tucks into the pike position, pats his belly bag, and disappears down his rappelling rope.

"Stupid bastard!" Harv, our spotter, reaches for the

radio. "Dispatch, Helicopter Five Hotel X-ray. Have visual of Incident One-Three-One with four souls left on board . . . make that three souls. Two. I take that back, one. Two sticks are planted. Only the short end still remains in the copter. Yes, they were told! Over."

The pilot muscles his body around, jams his finger into the pine-tree logo on my jacket. "You stay put." He grabs the radio, and I step out onto the skids.

I have no authority to leave this copter. I have to stay. Mox will get a hand slap when he returns. But maybe not me. I could get the superintendent's boot.

"Jake!" Koss's voice is thin and distant.

"Guess it is our war," I say to Harv. "Later."

Finding our safety zone. Securing the eighty-pound K-bag filled with saws and food, axes and survival equipment. There will be time for all that. But not now. I stand on the skid and stare out over the sea of green. Smoke rises from beneath the canopy of trees and sends spindly fingers up to grab me. It's down there, waiting to destroy or be destroyed.

I glance at the tail rotor. No use waiting for Harv's signal. It won't come. My heartbeat races, and a smile so big I feel it spreads across my face. The smoke, it comforts me, and I remember camping trips with Dad.

"Jake!"

I zip down the line into the suffocating cloud. My feet hit Koss's hands, and I hear curses and laughter. I slow. We descend together. The thicker the smoke, the clearer I think. The cloud that fogs my mind blows away, and I'm all here. Right now. Let there be light.

We drop into the furnace and this hell's hazy glow. Feet hit the logging road at the canyon's bottom.

"Glad you joined us, kid." Mox smiles.

My eyes scan for safety zones—alternative spots to flee into, and I see none. *There's only the road. This is off to a great start!*

"Gentlemen." Mox points toward a wall of fire that stretches up one side of the canyon. "That is not our fire. Our fire is two miles over that ridge. Ten minutes ago, this fire didn't exist. But Immortals are always in the right place at the right time."

I turn from the blaze and bombs and falling trees.

Behind me, an untouched forest, dark and beautiful, stretches up toward the opposite peak.

"If this fire makes here, we'll lose her. She'll jump the road." Moxie races twenty feet toward the blaze. "Here! This old fire line. She stops here. Widen it!"

I grab my cutter and rip the cord. The wind blows steady from the west, smacks the fire in the face. Chainsaws roar and eat up anything the fire might find tasty.

We whack brush in the black, on the tarry patch of earth consumed before the wind forced her back.

The heat is unbelievable.

"Whew," I say. "She's hot."

Koss turns his sooty face. His eyes dance. "And dirty. Kick."

I kick at the ground brush and overturn fresh tinder. "We're too close."

A breeze, gentle and scorching, licks my lips. A northern breeze. Koss freezes. He knows it, too. Wind shift. Dirty burn. It's not done with this charred ground.

"Hey, Koss," I yell. "That breeze is circling—"

"Moxie!" Koss hollers. "What do you think about Chinese for dinner tonight?"

"Ask Fatty!"

"Mexican." Fatty's voice sounds thin, far away.

"Would you consider Chinese made by Mexicans?" Koss checks the wind, peeks back at me. "Stay close!" He moves forward.

"How come Chinese food is the only thing not made in China?" Mox hollers.

Koss laughs, wild and free. "You're in the great state of California, my friend."

I can't see anyone but Koss through the smoke, but I don't need to. Moxie's, Fez's, and Fatty's chainsaws snarl in the distance. Hanging branches, fire food to the treetops, lie in piles on the ground. Fez's handiwork. Fatty and Koss clear brush and saw anything that still stands.

We wind through Snake Valley. Another north wind blasts; heat singes my eyebrows. We're too close.

Moxie is playing again.

"Fall back, Mox!" I rasp, and gulp water from my canteen.

Twenty paces ahead a charred ponderosa pops and explodes with a shower of embers. A second more, and another blows. Trees creak, fall. Koss turns and grimaces. A nightmare has begun.

"Make the road, Jake, dump your gear, and tent up like a turtle. This will be close!" Koss ditches his saw and claws at his survival tent. I drop my pack and run. Ahead, across the trail, embers ignite into fireballs and creep up fuel ladders toward the sky. She's jumped the road.

Cut off from Moxie, Fez, and Fatty, I fall to my knees.

"Your shelter, asshole!" Koss hollers. "Get up. She's blowin' over. Now! Now!"

I look over my shoulder, see his black outline pull his head into his tent. I stagger to my feet and gasp onto the trail. I stare up the west side toward the ridge. In the fire's light, I catch a silhouette against the burgundy sky. A home with a play set. The wind whips, crazed, deciding whose side it's on. And shifts. East, straight east.

Oh, please, no.

More fireballs hurtle into fresh tinder. That house has five minutes, tops.

"No one said there was a house!" I shout. "Mox, nobody briefed us on the house!"

I clamor up toward the hot spots, stomp and snuff and hack.

"Deploy shelters!" Mox's voice is faint.

"No!" I stare at the house, climb above the new burn, and start to clear. Three hacks with my ax, and a projectile lodges between my shoulder blades. I'm face in the dirt.

"Get into your damn shelter!" Koss rips the canister off my back.

I roll over and kick him hard in the chest. "The house!"

Back on me, he rips off my goggles, backhands me, and I see double. The world flips, and he presses my face into the earth, ups the tent, squeezes me inside. The material over me heats up, and I hear him curse outside. Then a crack, and the tent glows orange.

"I burn!" he screams, thuds to the ground.

Koss is not five feet outside my lifesaver. The air inside of my tent scorches my lungs. It's a burnover.

For minutes, I cover my head and whimper, try to
mute the sound of death around me. It sounds strangely
beautiful. Not a roar. Just a gentle surrender of a forest
to the monster—a crackle and a hiss and a voice. Koss.

"You're a good kid, Jake." He coughs, whispers, "Get
as far from Mox as you can. Tell Rose I love her." A
choke of air catches in his throat, and he exhales slowly.
"And kill the Rush Club."

A shudder ripples my shelter. Another wind shift.
An hour later, I squeeze out. Mox, Fez, and Fatty stand
around Koss, charred, half inside his tent.

I retch and look away. Fine mist from a water tanker
above coats my face, and the forest hisses around me.

Mox looks toward the sky and takes the mist full on.
Mud and grime smudge his face. He kneels over Koss,
whispers, "It was Jake, you know that, don't you?" He
stands, nudges Koss's body with his boot. Mox's black-
ened jaws tighten and twitch. His gaze finds me, pierces
me; it would kill me if it could. "Okay, guys." He wipes
his eye with the heel of his hand. "Let's do Chinese
tonight."

***

I SIT IN A DAZE while the crew reports in the base manager's office. I nod every time I hear my name. After hundreds of nods, he lets me go. The others walk to the villa to clean up.

I walk across town.

I pound on Salome's door. Mrs. Lee opens and gasps.

"Oh, dear Lord, are you all right?" She reaches for my ripped sleeve, but I pull away, swallow hard.

"Salome," I whisper. "I need her. Is she at Mid Cal?"

"No. She's back this weekend for services. She's at the church this evening, dear. Come in." She reaches for my arm. "Let me get you to a doc—"

I watch her grab and pull as if I'm somebody else. "What day is it?"

"Sunday, of course." A look of fear crosses her face. "Stay here. I'll get Jacob."

My mind clouds over, and I stumble backward down the step. I can't stay, here or anywhere.

There was a house. Houses mean kids. I grab my hair and pull.

Her name is Rose. I know her like I knew Koss. They met twelve years ago while dancing and have been dancing ever since. I've seen pictures. She's beautiful. And alone.

I walk away.

I wander the outskirts of town to Brockton Baptist. I go to be near her, to fill the guilty cracks of my mind with the thought of her. I circle the church and listen to them sing. The building is large and old and imposing, with doors so huge, no kid could open them.

They'll be finished soon, and I circle again, pause at the steps.

No more waiting.

Up the steps. Through the doors. I stand on the inside. I cross through an empty entryway toward the big room, where 150 heads bow.

I slip into the backseat and fill the sanctuary with the scent of death. Across the aisle a woman gasps. Mrs. Ramirez. Heads turn one by one, and I scan. Third row center, Salome's eyes widen. She stands and walks down the aisle. She reaches me, grabs my collar, and tugs. I rise and follow.

She drags me into daylight, reaches out, and strokes the singed portions of my sleeves. *Keep doing that.* My heartbeat slows. Then I remember.

"I killed him. I killed Koss."

She stares and steps forward, buries herself in my smoky chest. We stand for minutes, and when she finally stops squeezing, I breathe deep.

"Let's walk." I say.

She nods.

We walk out of Brockton. The story comes out in short bursts. By the time we reach Northwest Gorge outside of town, I'm getting tired. I barely have enough strength to crawl up beneath the crumbling train trestle. We huddle together; she strokes my head, and I collapse into her lap.

"You know how to use that shelter." Her hands are soft and perfect, and I'm so tired. "Why didn't you crawl in yourself?"

I cough hard. "The house. The house had a light on. It had a play set in back."

It's silent.

"You can't keep doing this to yourself," Salome says.

I lift my head, stare into my best friend's eyes. "Tell me how to stop."

CHAPTER 21

I WAKE UP HUDDLED BENEATH Salome's jacket. She sits some feet off, writing in her journal.

"You've scribbled in that since we were five. Don't you run out of sheets?"

She slams it shut, smiles. "How long have you been awake?" She scoots toward me.

I shake my head. "Why?"

"I was just praying, that's all."

"God tell you anything?"

"No."

I push up onto my feet. "He never will. Something inside you knows that."

Salome starts to speak, but I interrupt. "And no. I don't want to get into this right now."

"You brought it up!"

"Did not."

"You asked if God told me—"

"I—I'm going for a swim."

Salome shrugs. "Have fun." She plucks her pen from the grass and licks its tip.

I scoot away, slide down the grassy embankment, and follow the winding trail down to the river. I strip down to my boxers and dive. Cold steals my breath, and I break the waterline, goose-bumped and chest pounding. Water swirls around massive boulders, rushes through frothy channels, and whips me downstream. I let it carry me into a giant chunk of stone. I find footing and climb up, watch the world spin wild and random around me.

Black smoke billows to the south, and the smell of death, hideous and sweet, tingles in my nose. Yesterday doesn't make sense. Koss shouldn't have died. He couldn't die. None of us can, not really.

Water splashes my body, and I feel small. I hate the feeling. Small feels weak—weak and stupid and helpless.

"Koss!" The rush of water swallows my loudest yell. I

can't even make a sound in this new world, where I sit, half naked and insignificant. I rub my hands over the boulder, feel the solid on my fingertips.

Salome!

A feeling, ugly and strong, grows in my gut. I don't know it. But it jitters and spreads to my brain like a virus. I push gently back into the stream, then thrash toward the riverbank. I run like a Neanderthal through the woods, find my clothes, and whip them on.

I crunch up the path, full of this tense, anxious thing that feels like death. *Be there, Salome.* Sweat drips down as I bound onto the embankment, crawl up to our crow's nest. *Please, be there—*

Salome.

"What's wrong?"

Her words are always like that—simple and perfect. I calm and shake my head. "You're still here."

"Have I ever left you?"

I close my eyes. "No."

Salome sets down her journal, glances up, stands, and takes my hand. She leads me to the top of the trestle. We look across the span—a hundred-yard tangle of rotten wood that trains used to trust—but not now. Five feet wide with no railing, a fall off the top and game's over.

I've crossed it only three times.

"You don't like it up here," I say.

"You have that right." She squeezes my hand. "But it's where you live. It's where Koss lived." She lets my hand go and takes a slow step onto the first rail. "It's where I have to go to reach you. It must be."

I watch her feet. She moves them slowly, as if they weigh a thousand pounds.

"What is it about this?" She says it like she knows. Salome takes another step. "Why push it?"

"That's not safe out there."

She takes another large step, and I wince. She's reached the Coffin Zone. The embankment below wouldn't catch her, she'd . . .

"Come on back." That jittery ugly thing bounces around inside my skin.

She turns. "Come get me."

I step out, not fast and strong, but cautious. Scared, scared of being scared. I reach out my hand. She doesn't take it.

"Yesterday, it could have been you. It could be me now." She glances down, and I see her blink hard, close her eyes, and waver.

"Get back!" I leap to her, gather her around the waist, and pull her off the trestle. We collapse onto the grass.

We stare at the sky. She's out of breath. I am, too.

"We're not immortal, are we?" I ask.

Salome winces and whispers, "You saw Koss lying there. Did he look it?"

I turn toward her and ball up, as small as I can get. My mind swirls like the water, and the cloud fills my thoughts. "Koss. And Drew."

"What are we doing, Jake? Are we lost?" Troy drops another pile of sunflower seeds on the forest floor.

"We'll follow the seeds out. Besides, I know exactly where I am. You got to see this. I found it yesterday . . . there it is!"

I take off running.

"Slow down! I can't drop seeds so fast—oh, wow."

Troy and I look up at the maze of ropes that crisscross the top of hundred-foot pines. It looks like a man-made spiderweb.

"Who would put ropes way up there?" he asks.

"Don't know. Let's go up and find out."

"No way. I'm not climbing up there."

"Okay. I'll tell you what's on top."

I ring the tree with the rope I brought and dig my baseball cleats into bark. I climb up lumberjack-style. Rope over rope, ten-year-old legs churn up to the first branch. From there it's easy. I climb from branch to branch, reach, and grope until I finally feel the first rope of the web.

"This is so cool!" I call down. "I'm going to climb across it to the other tree!"

He stands. "Come down! Mom said I need to be home by supper!"

"We will!"

I make my way out onto the rope web, look down at the ground below. Halfway across, I freeze. I stare into eyes that don't stare back. Salome's older brother, Drew, hangs there, fifty feet up, a rope tangled around his waist and another around his neck.

I inch closer. "Drew? Can you hear me?" I start to cry. "Why are you up here?"

His body gently twists. I can't touch it.

I stare a long time.

Now Drew's lifeless face morphs into Koss's and springs to deadly life.

"Kill the Rush Club."

My breath catches, and I exhale hard, but the smell— I can't describe it.

"I said, did they look it?" Salome repeats.

"No, but Koss . . . I couldn't see him, but I heard him. He told me to kill the Rush Club."

She tenses. "Was Drew part of this club?"

I have no proof. I don't have the one answer she

wants more than any other in this world. But I have an idea.

"I think so."

"Are you?"

"Not yet. I haven't been invited. I haven't spun yet. I think I took the first step. I took the jacket."

She picks a flower and spins the stem between her fingers. "How's that going for you?"

"Don't think I can wear it anymore."

Salome stands. "Then right now I'll say what I didn't before. Get out. Get out of this town. You might make it to twenty. You might actually live."

I stand, brush the grass off my grimy jumpsuit. Had I not heard Koss, had he not spoken outside my survival tent, maybe I could've quit. But he did. And he spoke to me—he always watched out for me. I didn't listen to him when I first arrived, but I will now. It's the least I can do. I'm not leaving this crew until the club is dead.

"Well?" she asks. "Can you leave?"

"I need to finish it off first. The less you know, probably the better. Inside my tent, I made Koss a guarantee. Don't think I could live with myself if I left now."

"Even now that you're a mere mortal?" She steps nearer.

I want it, that peaceful thing that rests inside of her,

that turns blue eyes into calm pools. I want it to blanket my confusion and make everything black and white like it is for her. It's right here in front of me, in her, but it's a world away.

Her eyes widen. Her gaze suddenly warms. "Let's escape. Let's go camping," she says. "I've been working too hard at school. I'll run home and tell my parents, and we'll take off."

I stare at her. She's never skipped out on anything.

"With Koss gone, our crew will be pulled and questioned more and . . . I should probably be here. I'm not certain what they do to people who take off."

Her face still beams. Responsibility used to get her every time. Not now.

"Don't you have stuff to do?" I swallow hard. "No plans with anybody?"

She smiles. "That depends on what you say next."

She's good. No, she's perfect.

"Yeah, let's go."

CHAPTER 22

IT'S TWO HOURS BEFORE SALOME returns, her oversize gym bag in hand. She bounces up to me, throws back her hair, and winks. "Let's get out of here."

We walk hand in hand, my fire gear slung over my shoulder.

"I was thinkin' you'd changed your mind," I say, and we hike toward the base and my waiting Beetle.

She laughs like she did years ago. "My dad would have liked that."

I freeze. "I don't want to mess up—"

She grabs my arm. "We just needed to have a little talk about trust."

"He doesn't trust me alone with you anymore?"

"Oh." Salome smiles and leans into me. "I think he trusts you just fine."

We reach the villa, exceptionally quiet today, as if the buildings themselves mourn.

I frown and hand her the keys. "Probably best if you pick up the car, in case the crew is wandering around the lot. I'll wait across from Randall's."

Minutes later, she appears, and I take her place behind the wheel.

We both know where we're going, though it's been years. We drive south, through the mountains where our crew dropped, where Koss dropped. Red-flag fire-risk warnings keep us on the alert, and a haze darkens the sun. Hours later, the breeze kicks up, the air clears, and my body relaxes. The smell of dead things vanishes, and the sound of Salome's laughter surrounds.

I love this drive. I love this drive with her. She rubs the tension from my shoulders, and I take long looks at my friend. So beautiful.

"What are you thinking?" she asks.

"Huh?"

"Right now. What are you thinking about?"

I swallow hard. "Things I can't say and things I can't do, and things I want to say and want to do."

She shifts in her seat. "Like what?"

The car eases itself onto the shoulder, and I sit and stare straight ahead.

Salome takes my hand. "Like what?"

She asked.

Koss is dead, a victim of getting too close to me. But I can't fight this right now.

I reach over and touch her lips. "That was the first thing."

Her lips part, kiss my fingers. "And then?"

My hand caresses her cheek, her neck, moves to her thigh. "I guess this is what came next."

"Were you ever thinking of this?"

Salome bends forward and brushes her lips across my ear, my cheek. She smiles and kisses my neck, gently bites my lip, and pulls away. For a moment, she is my world. I am perfect; my heart thumps perfectly. We are perfect. And we kiss.

We draw together and stay that way. My hands, usually wandering during a kiss, tremble against her back.

Minutes later she pulls back and breathes deep. I blink hard.

"Honestly, I hadn't let myself think that far ahead," I say.

"That's one of the irritatingly wonderful things about

you." She rests her head on my shoulder. "I know I'd always be safe with you."

Salome's never wrong. Except now. Especially now. I know two things: I'm totally confused, and she's never been in more danger.

WE GET TO MY DAD'S MOUNTAIN—Hank's Hill. The name fits because Dad owns the whole thing. It was a gift for Mom. Not many guys would think to buy their wives a mountain; hand it to Dad, he thinks big. Tree-lined at the bottom, the top is covered with wildflowers and scrubby bushes. It's what Mom loved. She'd come here to paint the sunrise. Sometimes the sunset. In the years before she left, only the sunset.

But years ago, before, the Lees would come with us to the hill. Once a month we'd pile into the shack Dad built smack on the top. No running water. No electricity. Just a view to kill for and a weekend laughing with friends. There was no better place to be.

Salome and I spent hours in search of "blue rocks." I've never found them anywhere else but on the plateau that forms the top of Hank's Hill. The rocks were opaque and blue like her eyes are blue. We collected them in a rock jar, planned on selling them for big money. We'd become wealthy rock salespeople.

The Beetle winds the thin strip of earth that snakes toward the top; the poor engine revs and whirs all the way.

"Get out and push, will ya?" I smile.

Salome throws open her door and unbuckles her belt.

"Hey!" I reach for her and grab her leg. "I'm kidding. I was only kid—"

She laughs at me; soon I laugh, too. We quiet and sit in comfortable silence—the kind you enjoy only with a friend who knows everything you've done, everything you desire. Well, almost everything.

My hand is still on her thigh. I grit teeth and force my fingers back to my side of the car.

Hands that took life shouldn't deserve this feeling.

CHAPTER 23

THE SHACK IS STURDY OAK and pine logs plugged with pitch. Weatherworn gray, it's as rustic as Dad's mill is lavish. A simple porch, one double-hung window. When I was growing up, it was a castle; Scottie and I were the kings, and Salome was our queen.

We climb the three steps, unlatch the door, and push inside. The smell of sweet earth says I'm home, and for a moment pushes out the awful.

Salome runs her hand along the sill. "It's been, what, eight years since we've been here? Since Drew died."

"Yeah, and Mom left." I frown and let my gaze wander. "Doesn't look eight years empty."

There's not a cobweb anywhere, and canned food is stacked neatly in the corner of the main room. I walk through to the bedroom tucked in back. It's clean with a pillow and a freshly made bed.

"Recent visitors," I say. "But there's only one way to be sure." Close in size to the bedroom, the outhouse stands fifty paces off the shack. I leave Salome, walk out back, pull the pin, and swing open the door. Toilet paper.

"So much for time alone," I mutter, and rejoin Salome. "Somebody has found really cheap rent. Doubt we'll be alone tonight." I toss my things into the open bedroom. "Let's wait and see who shows."

Salome raises an eyebrow. "As long as you see them first."

We plunk onto the porch and stare at the sky and at each other. A feeling grows and grows and draws me to her. When I watch her tongue gently touch her teeth enough times, or replay our time in the car, I know she burns inside. But her words stay innocent and safe— things I no longer am.

Inside, the monster awakens. First with a yawn, then a stretch, then a roar. It doesn't like to be denied and searches for a rush.

"I can't sit around." My mind races. "The gulley." I

decide aloud. "Remember it? I wonder if I could still ride it down."

Salome leans into me. "It's eating you again."

I know what I've done with that one kiss. This half expression of what I want—it's killing me. I now live in this horrible middle place where I can, but I can't, and nothing will be the same. I've felt. I've tasted. Like a drunk condemned to life in a bar, I now must live inches from my addiction and fill the urge with something else.

I fall across her lap, and she pats my shoulder. "Okay," she says. "The gulley."

I leap up, dash inside, and dig in the closet. I yank out the rusted wooden sled by the hand brakes. My chest aches, and I push outside. "Can you believe the sled was still there?" Salome isn't where I left her, and I walk the porch, the sled's runners thumping against the wooden floor slats. "Salome?"

"I'm over by the trench!" She stands in the distance, her fingers locked behind her head, and stares over the hill's lip.

Cleared of rocks, the gulley extends down the mountain to the tree line. Like a bobsled course at the Olympics, it's steep and winding and unforgiving. As a child, I spent hours digging and smoothing and racing down the mini-gorge.

"Step back." I jog to her and point the sled down the hill. "I won't be long."

She plops on the front of the sled. "This is our time. We do this together."

I stare at her back, her trusting back, and ease down behind her. My arms and legs straddle her body; I feel her warmth.

"I'll never let anything happen to you, do you know that?" I ask.

"I do." She ducks her head. "Tell me when it's over."

This is so wrong. My brain sucking Salome into my world. But nothing will touch her. I would die before that.

I push off. We gain speed instantly and hurtle down the trench. We weave, and I bend and hold Salome tight. She does not scream. She trusts, which is worse than a scream.

But I see, and what I see is wonderful and terrifying. The bottom fast approaches. The gulley once banked to the left to form a gentle stop, but the turn is now a rock wall, a mound of sediment built up from years of rain.

"Don't look!" Pebbles pepper my face and sting like a thousand needle jabs.

She turns and yells. "I'm not!"

I dig in the left brake, and we bank up the side and

out of the trench. Speed carries us on toward the tree line. We won't survive.

"On my word, lean backward!"

She nods. "It's bumpier! What happened?"

"Now!"

I wrap arms around her and tug. Chipped rock sets my back on fire, but I wince, lift my rear, and let the sled race on ahead. I am now the sled, the heels of my boots chattering, grinding us to a halt. Behind me, where my back should be, I feel only pain. Not pain on skin, just pain. The skin is gone. But Salome is still on top, safe in my arms.

We stop, and I groan.

"I'm opening my eyes now. Oh, Jake!" She scrambles off. "There's blood around you—"

"Tell me you're okay," I whisper.

"Turn over!"

"Say it."

"I'm okay. Now turn over before I slug you!"

I roll slow. "How bad?"

She gasps, swallows, and clears her throat.

"It'll hurt a lot more when I'm done digging out the stones. Stay here." Salome scampers around Hank's Hill. She's gone for a long time, and I sit up, then try to stand. But my feet slip, and I land hard on my side, groan, and stay down.

I bake in the sun, feel the hill move beneath me.

Then her voice, gentle. "Up we go."

Soon I lie in bed, while Salome digs in my back with her tweezers. I focus on her hand on my head, separate myself from my own body. It's the only way not to scream.

Finally, the tweezers plop onto the bedside table.

"I think that's most of the big ones," she says.

"Seemed a good idea at the time," I say, and roll onto my side.

Salome stands and gives a puff into her bedroll. "I bet they all do." She sighs and kisses my cheek. "That's for watching out for me." She winds up and belts my shoulder. "That's for almost killing you."

CHAPTER 24

NOBODY COMES DURING THE NIGHT. I get up in the morning, put on a loose shirt. It feels remarkably good. I feel remarkably good, considering the last days. The guilt over Koss has ebbed from a tidal wave to a lapping, slow and constant. This, I think, is due to her. If one thing separates Salome from the rest of world, it's that she does not blame.

I find her on the porch, still and deep in thought.

"Mornin'," I say.

She lifts strands of blond over her ears, and the day gets brighter.

"How's the backside today?"

"Oh, it's been better. I, uh—" I plunk down beside her. "Our little slide down memory lane was really stupid."

She nods slowly. "What's stupid, what's needed; it's hard to tell the difference with you." She points. "Do you see that brook down there? Isn't it beautiful?"

"Yeah."

Salome opens her mouth, changes directions, and chuckles. "I've decided. Today, I'm in charge. I'm in charge of what we do. I'm in charge of where we go. Everything is up to me." She flashes a look I've seen on her mother. "You have no say in the matter."

I grin, feel a searing across my shoulder blades, then grimace. "No say. Got it. Where to first?"

"I'll be honest." She scoots away, faces me, and rests her head in one hand. "The reason I wanted you here is because I don't want you there. I want you off Mox's team and preferably out of this town."

"It's not so simple anymore—"

"This is a shut-up moment. You have no say."

I slap my hand over my mouth.

"But here's my problem, mine and yours. You think the only way to live, the only way to lift that cloud fuzzing your head, is to walk Mox's death tightrope. I don't like the option, but ever since you joined the feds, that crew is the only light you see. Since you need that adrenaline boost to feel sane, it would seem that Mox and his insane Immortals are a perfect fit."

She straightens her legs and lifts her arms in a full-body stretch. Makes me want to hold her.

"So there's the problem I've been thinking about for, well, months."

"I don't think we'll have this problem forever. There are things you don't—"

Salome places her hand over my mouth. I raise my hands.

"So I need to convince you that you *can* feel alive when you're not floating in caves or embedding rocks into your back."

She throws back her hair, and her voice strengthens. "You irritate me, Jake King. I have one regret from last year. My prom. I waited all year for my senior prom. I waited for my neighbor to ask me, but the idiot was busy preparing for immortality by jumping out of airplanes."

"Wait—"

She slugs me. "Yes, airplanes. Meanwhile, my dress, my beautiful green dress, hung laughing at me. Four guys, stable, considerate, on-the-ground guys, asked me to go. Four! Four times I said no. Well, today you will finally ask me. So ask!"

"Is this an excuse to whack me?"

"Ask!"

"Um, Salome, would you like to go to the prom with me?" I scratch my chin. "How was that?"

"Wonderful. And I would absolutely love to!" She jumps up, runs inside, and brings out a crinkled green dress. "It got messed up in the bag, but I'm not going to let your months in smoke-jumper training destroy my senior prom."

She's joking, I see it in her face. But the words hurt because they're true.

Salome looks at me. It's a wide look that could mean anything. "What's the matter?" She fiddles with the dress in her hands. "You don't want to take me?"

"That's not it. I've messed up everything."

"Then today," she says, "make it right." Her voice lowers. "Please."

I slap my thigh, jump up, and wince from the pain in my back. "Yeah." I gain steam. "Yeah! I'll give you a prom to remember, my beautiful neighbor." I frown, stroke my loose T-shirt. "Hmm. Can't wear this to prom. Let's head to town."

We drive down into Mandre. Bar, gas station, super-ette. That's it. No way I'll find a suit in this speck of a town.

"We'll need to head to Holdingford for your suit," she says.

"Holdingford?" The vise on my lungs tightens. "Rose." Koss's fiancée, Rose, lives in Holdingford.

"Don't worry," Salome says. "I'm sure they'll have a flower shop."

Then it hits. The lunacy of it. All the horror and sadness and loss of the blaze, all the hope and joy and anticipation of my neighbor squeezed into these days. And in the middle—me—responsible for it all.

I peek at Salome. She beams. I can't take today away from her. Not now.

We enter Holdingford and shoot the day spending what little money I have. Tuxedo, corsage, food for the evening, music for the dance. Salome has her hair done; I get mine cut. And everywhere I listen for the name Rose. Because Koss is why I'm still here; he's the one who pushed us over the edge.

I wonder if Rose even knows.

We return to the shack with the sun screaming at our backs. My date lays out my clothes on the porch and bounces inside. "Knock in an hour."

"An hour?"

"Don't even try to figure it out. You're a guy." She shuts the door.

I glance at the tuxedo. A monkey suit for a monkey boy. I dress and wonder about the fire. Does it still burn? Did it reach the house? Is the department looking for me? Mox surely didn't take any credit for what happened. And what business does a killer have dressed like this? Doing prom with a girl like Salome? I touch my boutonniere and close my eyes. I see it burn. Flower, stem. Then my tux. But I don't feel it.

Left alone, thoughts flood. *I shouldn't be here. I should be taking my punishment. I—*

Behind me, a throat clears, and the shack door slams shut. I check my watch. I'm late.

I rise and knock.

"Be right down!" she calls.

"Down? Hey, I have to talk to you! Open the ____"

The door swings, and Salome stands before me. Shoulders tan and beautiful, eyes sparkling. She's a magnet. She erases every thought from my mind, and I step closer. My hands reach out and caress her waist. I swallow, puff out air, and pull my hands back.

"I'm sorry. It's just. You're absolutely gorgeous."

She lifts my chin. "No need to apologize. Are you ready?"

"For anything."

***

"TAKE A LEFT AT THE CORNER."

I frown at my date. "You sure?"

"Now take the next right."

"But—"

"Pull in."

I slow the car and breathe deep. We cross beneath the wrought-iron arch and roll to a stop. I played here when I was young, leaped from stone to stone, but the ground feels different now—more sacred, like Dad said it would one day. I set out and wade through the tall grass, to where I remember rests the first stone marker. I bend and swat away brush until my hand grazes cool granite. I trace the date with my pointer. 1935. HE FOUGHT BRAVELY.

The firefighters' graveyard is the reason Dad bought this hill. There were many other mounds available, in better locations along the ocean. But none of them came with this memorial. Thirty-plus markers to unknown men who died in the Pasquat Blaze of '35.

It's too soon, Koss's death too fresh, and my stomach turns.

I gesture around the place with my arms. "This is where you want to go on your prom night? There were plenty of restaurants in Holdingford."

She reaches into the car, and John Lennon floods the cemetery with "Imagine."

"Will you dance with me?" she asks.

"Here?" I look around. "It doesn't seem right, us dancing on top of all them."

"Will you dance with me?" She reaches out a hand, and I take it. We find an open spot. She lifts my hands, places them on her shoulders, and grabs my lapels. "Look at me."

I am. There's no way to avoid it. Her eyes capture, and the stones behind her fade away.

I pull her close, and she rests her head on my chest. My hands move over her bare back. Every part of me comes to life.

"So how about now?" she says. "What do you want to do right now?"

My mind swims. "Why do you keep asking me that? It's not obvious?"

"Many things have been obvious these last ten years . . . Do you like it here in my arms?"

"Yeah."

"How about your body and that unique brain of yours? Do they feel alive?"

"Yeah."

"And how's the weather inside?" She taps my temple. "Partly cloudy?"

"Clear. Warm. It's sure pleasant enough."

We sway in the headlights and listen to the breeze whistle through the graveyard. The music stopped long ago, but there's no need for beat, for rhythm. We fit. We flow. We belong.

"I want us to be together," she whispers. "If you stay with Mox . . . I know you. You'll push, and I'll get a call like we did with Drew." She swallows hard. "It'll be you this time. And I couldn't bear to lose both of you."

I glance around and hug tighter.

"Do you want to be one of these stones?" she continues. "Do you want to be where I'm not?"

I shake my head. She's right. I see it all. I see where it's going.

"So, friend, prom date, what will you do?" she asks.

Here's when I should tell her that I've thought about her since, well, forever. I should tell her why I've held her away. Why I've been afraid. I should let her into my world. All the way in. Right now, I know, Salome is my rush and always has been. I could find happiness. Maybe even peace.

But there's a knife that twists in my gut, the stabbing from a blade held by Koss's last words.

I shuffle my feet and run hands through my hair.

I have to stay in a little longer. But I can't disappoint her tonight.

"I'll leave. I'll tell Mox when I get back."

Salome grabs my cheeks and pulls my gaze into hers. "Give me your guarantee."

I'm screwed. "You got it."

She hugs me. I feel like a loser.

We finish the dance. Salome whirls and laughs. I grin—I've never seen her so happy, but when I pull her close, when my face is shielded from her gaze, my grin falls. To keep my friend's smile, I must ignore Koss's final wish.

The wind dies, and I slump toward the car. I feel Salome's gaze land heavy on my back.

"Only one dance?" she asks.

I rub my eyes. "After I quit . . . let's think here. What else am I gonna do?" I peek at her, her arms limp at her sides. I'm doing it again. Ruining her second prom. "But I know it's right. I mean, you make sense."

"I want to do more than just make sense." She approaches.

I nod. "You do."

We get back into the Beetle and drive up the hill in silence. An old truck is parked out front of the shack. I crunch to a stop. "Stay here. I'll get rid of them."

I hop out of the car, step quietly onto the porch, and throw open the door.

A scream, followed by fast Spanish. A woman gathers two children to herself. All I see are silhouettes and the whites of their eyes in the moonlight. The woman says nothing.

"English?"

She shakes her head.

I nod, lift up my hands. "Stay."

I turn and pause. I glance back at the girls, at the beautiful necklaces strung around their necks. Blue rocks.

I point to the girls, gesture toward their necks. Mom speaks quickly, starts to remove the strung stones. I wave my hands.

"No. You can keep them." I smile. I lift hands to the sky and shrug. "Where did you find them?"

She points to the closet. I open the door. In the dim light, there is a flash of blue from a jar on the floor. Our jar sparkles. Half full. I reach in and grab a few handfuls. It feels like I'm touching something precious, holy, I guess. I stuff my pockets with blue rocks and leave.

Outside, Salome lifts her head, eyes full of worry.

"It's a woman and a couple small kids," I say. "Gotta let them stay."

Salome nods. "I'll get our things." She disappears into the shack, appears a few minutes later.

"What about us?" she asks. "I don't want to go back. Not yet."

Her face glows smooth and light beneath the moon. It's no fair to look as she does. Not fair to me.

"I got a question," I say. "Seeing as we're not really neighbors right now—"

She raises her eyebrows.

I squirm. "I mean, yeah, we're neighbors, or at least were and this is your prom and all . . ."

"Go on."

"And to make it a real prom, I'm thinking, well . . ."

I kiss her. Full and rich and real. A breeze blows, swirls gentle around us. It touches every part of her body and vanishes into the night. But I get to stay and caress her arms and neck. I hear my name melt my ear, feel her lips turn mine to Jell-O. Knees weaken, and there's a good chance I'll go down, but not without her. Nowhere without her. She knows me and still she kisses me, and inside hope wakes up. She kisses me new.

We stumble toward the car with bodies locked. I fumble with the door, throw it open, and we ease into the front seat. My fingers stroke her hair, her shoulders, her back. They move toward the zipper, inch it down. Salome whispers, "Jake."

I pull back breathless and stare wild-eyed. "I'm sorry. I can't. I shouldn't. I'm so sorry."

She strokes my chest and whispers, "Why can't you ever shut up." Salome draws closer.

But I can't. My mind clouds. I swore I wouldn't let anything happen to her, not ever. I can't lose her.

"What's wrong?" She straightens.

"It means too much, you know? Too much. If you were somebody else . . . If you were Brooke, no problem, but you're not."

All warmth seeps from the car, and she wriggles away from me and into her seat. She flattens her dress and puffs out air.

I sit by a stranger. Salome stares straight ahead. I am alone and desperate. "Talk to me."

She doesn't move. "Take me home."

There's quiet, and there's something deeper. More than no noise, it's no possibility of noise. We drive back to Brockton in that hideous vacuum.

I pull into the Lees' driveway. "I'll do what I said."

She nods, looks down. "Do whatever you need to. Do what you want." Salome gets out, walks slowly toward the house.

"Hey!" I holler. "Sorry about messing up your prom."

She pauses, raises a hand, but doesn't turn.

CHAPTER 25

I SPEND THE NIGHT in my car in front of the villa, and wake up with my back on fire.

Two things I know.

Life is miserable without Salome, and I destroy whomever I touch.

I need to apologize, or at least string more painful words together.

I drive to the Lees'. My legs usually lighten as they walk up her driveway, but not now. Whatever went horribly wrong with her adds weight to my feet.

My hand suspends in midair, preknock. Mrs. Lee throws open the door.

Her gaze wanders over my wrinkled tuxedo, comes to rest on my boutonniere. She reaches out and unpins my limp flower.

"Come in, Jake."

She leads me to the living room, where we both sit on couches and say nothing. But her face seems fixed and unreadable, as if she has plenty to say. The silence kills me, and slowly I rise to my feet.

"I said some things, and I need to see—"

"She's back at school." Mrs. Lee looks down, clasps and unclasps her hands. "She's hurt."

"I know." In my heart, I feel a snap. "I need to speak with her in person so . . . uh . . ."

She doesn't respond, so I say good-bye and let myself out. I jog back to the Beetle and hit the gas.

Last year, we visited this campus often. I know it, know where she is. In the turret room in the mansion-like stone building on University Avenue. She always said she wanted to live there, and she can talk her way into any place.

I squeal to a stop in front of the mansion, run up the porch, and knock. Two girls throw open the door, raise their hands to their mouths, and break out laughing.

"Rough night, huh?" Left Girl says, reaches out her hand. "Maybe I can help."

I stare at her face. "Salome Lee. Is she here?"

Left looks at Right, and both lose their smiles. "Upstairs." They gesture toward the stairs.

I nod, push between them, and bound upward. Three staircases later, I throw open the turret door.

"You didn't give me much chance to explain—"

Beautiful arms I know wrap around broad shoulders I know. The kiss ends. Scottie turns, and our gazes lock.

I'll kill him.

Salome runs her hands over her thighs, then through her hair. "Jake, I—"

I turn and race down the stairs, split Ms. Left and Ms. Right, and sprint to my car. I dig frantically for my keys, yank them out, and whip them across the road.

My hand comes down on the hood, dents, aches, and comes down again.

I race to find my keys. My angry search is filled with curses, and I rage in the grassy field in which they landed.

"Jake!"

I ignore her, search on.

"Please, Jake. I want to talk to you."

I see a glint, grab the key ring, and storm toward the car.

"Go on, Salome. Go stick your face on my brother."

"Who gave you the right to control my life? You shut up. You shut your mouth."

"Done." I jump in, slam the door, jam the key into the ignition, and squeal away. I look in the rearview. Salome kneels on the grass; Scottie leans over her.

I want to crush something, because something in me is crushed. Salome can kiss anyone she wants. But she just kissed me.

I hate Scottie.

I drive fast and hard and squeal into Brockton. I pant and screech to a halt at the YMCA gym. I don't know how I got here, only that I need to move something heavy, something Scottie heavy. I need to force a 205-pound something into the air, and scream at it again and again.

I pound inside and make for the locker room. I smash shut my locker, kick the door open, and stomp into the Y's weight room. And freeze. Mox and Fatty and Fez high-five on the far side of the gym. Mox and Fez grab a fistful of Fatty's belly, laugh and joke and stare into the mirrors.

I walk in, take hold of Mox's shoulder, and spin him. His eyes grow big, then turn to slits. He reaches for my hand, vise-grips it, and tries to peel it free, but my fingers aren't moving. I grab his other shoulder and squeeze. I squeeze until his face twitches and his knees buckle.

"Tell me why you left Koss and me on that last drop. I'm losing everything. Everyone. Since finding out about the Rush Club, life's . . . been . . . torture." I topple him onto the mat and stumble backward. Everyone stares at me.

Mox massages his arms, stands slowly. "How does it feel to kill a man? To be the reason Koss is dead." He breathes in deeply. "To breathe air and know that your father should be mourning. What does that feel like?"

"I—I didn't mean—"

"You didn't mean to hurt him?" Mox slowly circles me. "You didn't mean to join my crew? What in your life do you mean to do?" He stops, leans in, and hisses. "Little victim."

I stagger out of the Y. There is an emptiness so big, I can't fill it. It's time to leave this town.

CHAPTER 26

SUITCASE FILLED, I TAKE ONE more look around the villa, at the wall I spray-painted, the red circle. I've now failed Salome *and* Koss. I'll leave alone, and the Rush Club will live on.

"What do you know?"

I glance back. The three stooges fill the front door. I ignore them.

Mox repeats, "I said, what—"

"Heard you the first time." I turn and look. He isn't so everything now. But neither am I.

"Before you run off again, would you be so kind as to tell me where you found out about the Rush Club."

He glances at the dried-blood circle on the wall. "Scottie? Troy?"

"I watched you emcee Troy's ceremony." I grab hooded pullovers from the front closet. "You kill firefighters. Don't know how you live with that."

"It's not that different from what you did," Mox hisses, tongues his cheek. "I don't force the spin on anyone. Face it. You have no idea why we do it." He winces and stretches his shoulder. "But you could."

I drop my suitcase.

Mox continues, "There's room for you."

"No. It's the rule. Only twenty."

Mox looks down. "Don't suspect he'll object now. You took care of that."

Fez eases up to Mox. "What are you thinking? You saw what he did."

I reach for my suitcase handle, then pause. My fingers stretch and ball into a fist.

Mox wants me dead. He hates me. He hates my being young. He hates my having been forced on his team. He hates my dad, my brother, and what I did to Koss.

I stare at his smirk. This isn't an offer. It's an opportunity for all that hate of his to come out.

"You want me in."

He smiles and says nothing.

Mox is playing. He rocks like he's close to a blaze. He wants to extinguish my life.

I straighten, face him square, and whisper, "You want me dead."

His lip curls up.

Join the Rush Club. Kill the Rush Club. My last chance to keep my guarantee.

"If you let me in, I'm coming after you." I say.

"I'd be disappointed if you didn't. So are you—"

"In."

Mox rounds my shoulder with his arm. Like Dad did at the administration building. Like Scottie did at the mill. Like Koss did on the trail and Salome did at the shack. But they're all gone. All of them. Only my would-be murderer remains in my world. An adrenaline junkie like me.

CHAPTER 27

"JAKE."

My eyelids shoot open, and I'm wide-awake. I needed a day to think of the right words to tell her, but she beat me to the deal. She's here. A quiet tap on the window. I flop over and jam my head under the pillow. A minute later, I poke out my head. The world is silent.

"Get out from beneath that pillow!" Her voice cuts into the room, grabs me by the neck, and yanks. I walk over to the glass and stare out at Salome, her hands cupped around her face.

Come with me, she mouths.

I let the shades clap down and turn back toward the bed.

More tapping. I whip on my clothes, pound out the door, and round the villa.

I glare at my best friend, say nothing to my best friend.

"Can we talk?" she asks.

"Depends on the topic."

"Fine," she says. "About what you saw—"

"How long you been seeing him?"

"That's not tonight's headline."

"Oh, I think it is. 'Girl Acts All into Jake, Runs Off with Brother.'"

"How about 'Stupid Guy So Blind He'll End Up with Brooke.'"

"I'm going to bed." I show her my back and take a step. My left foot snags on her shoe, flies up, and I flop onto the ground.

She kicks my thigh. "No, you're coming with me."

I scowl at my tripper. She's beautiful. I hate that about her.

"You left me." I push up to a kneel. "I needed you, and you left me."

"You don't need me." She walks toward her waiting

car, looks over her shoulder, and gestures. I rise and join her, climb into her car. Together we speed out of Brockton.

"We've got a long way to go together." Salome looks over. "So maybe it's best if you don't speak. It'll keep you from saying something stupid."

"Where we going?"

She says nothing.

"I'll play along, just don't take me to your boy-friend."

Tires squeal. "You can't keep that mouth shut. I warned you." She grabs my ear. "Scottie's not my boy-friend. And if he was, would that bother you?"

I reach up, free my lobe from her pinchers. "Not at all," I lie.

Salome leans back and breathes deep. "Mom was right."

"About—"

"Everything."

HOURS LATER WE REACH OUR destination, the town of Canton, specifically the brick house with a twelve-foot metal sculpture dominating the front yard. I named it the *Weeping Rose*. The sculpture is alive with flowers that cascade down from the multiple beds built into it. I remember hauling junk with Salome from the salvage yard to Mom's place. We dumped it on her lawn and she made it into something beautiful.

I follow Salome out of the car and into the backyard. Mom's home sits on a private pond. She has a tiny dock and a hidden patio littered with sculptures and statues. And on that dock sits a small person on the one small lawn chair.

I know her. I know her from behind and in the dark and from a distance. I know her and love her and quicken steps toward her.

My feet pound the deck boards. She jumps up, and I freeze.

There are things I want to say now, words that should fall from my mouth and surround my mom. I want to tell her everything that's happened these last months, but I can't. It's not where we're at anymore. Though my mind is clear, I stand and stare at someone I know less each time I visit.

"Jake," she says, and buries her hands in her pockets. "It's been a long time."

Her voice peels years from me, and I feel ten years old again. I hate that.

"Too long," I say, and jam my hands in my pockets, too. "How are you?"

"I'm feeling much better. In fact, I told Scottie—"

I straighten. "Is he here? Where is he?" I push away from Salome and storm toward the back porch.

Mom calls gently, "Why are you mad at your brother?"

I pause and throw my arms in the air. "Doesn't matter. He wins again."

Mom approaches me from behind, strokes my head, and continues on around toward the front of the house. "Let's walk."

I lock my fingers behind my head and exhale hard. My legs feel like lead. But Salome nods gently, and I follow my mom.

We walk in silence, twice circling the neighborhood. The third time around, Mom presses into my shoulder. I stare down at her.

"Why didn't you call these last months?"

"Of course, that's the question you should ask." Mom's voice wavers. "Scottie told me you were rappelling and making new friends. I didn't want to intrude."

I breathe deep. "Isn't that a mom's job?"

"And, I suppose, you could have called me? Your e-mails are always so short."

"Things are complicated." I exhale. "I'm into stuff that needs working out. Doesn't make it right, though."

A burn ignites in my gut. "Is that how things were for you when you left? Just too complicated?"

I shoot Mom a glance. She faces me, but her gaze can't stick, and it falls to the pavement.

"I wasn't well, Jake. Up here." She touches her head. "I felt so overwhelmed. I was frozen." She slows way down. "I needed to escape, maybe not so unlike you. So I used art. And you have your own wild trapdoor to freedom."

I see it now. I see the replays of Mom years ago, the feeble mom I knew I needed to protect, but didn't know the enemy. I see her trembling and remember sitting on her lap, turning the pottery wheel. The kitchen, my kitchen, and weeks of mac and cheese as she lay on the couch. It didn't seem strange then; it was life and Dad's absences were normal fireman behavior.

Another bump on the shoulder. "I was nothing for your father. I had nothing to give him."

"You're my mom."

She steps in front of me. "And I'm so proud of you." Mom kisses my cheek.

"Sure you don't mean Scottie? He hasn't been expelled, or—"

"He has been a help since he's moved in . . . He loves you," she says.

"He loves Salome."

"Yes. Is there a problem with that?"

"Yeah."

"You don't own her affections. Did you think you two would stay kids forever?"

"No."

"Well then, my grown son, why not make a new start with a new crew? Maybe you could end up at that smoke-jumping base you wrote me about? I think it's time for you to leave Brockton."

You've been talking to Salome.

"You and Dad agree on something. He wants me to leave, too."

Mom smiles. "Wouldn't that be wonderful? You and Salome both doing what you love?"

"It would."

I FIND SALOME SITTING on the dock, her knees drawn up to her chest. The moon shimmers, and she searches out over the water.

"Why did you bring me here?" I ask.

"You don't see it. You don't see that there are places outside Brockton where people love you. Unless you're out of town, you can't see it clear . . . You don't need them—the Immortals."

I squat down next to her. "No. But they need me. Because I thought of a way to stop the club. I can take it apart. I can make it so nobody ever gets hurt by Mox again. And I'm the only one who'll do it."

Salome stretches out her legs, dips her feet in the water. "And what happens to you?"

"I don't know." I lift my eyebrows. "But when this is done, when I've all the information I need, will you help me kill the club? Will you write it up? Splash it in big letters in that college newspaper you write for. Nobody will ignore it then."

"Jake, I've been waiting on you for what seems like a lifetime. I get what you're doing. It's only that . . ."

I cock my head.

"I need you to come back for me. Once you do whatever hideous thing you have to do for the club, you'll leave, right?"

"I'll be back, Sal."

"You'll be free to fight fire anywhere. Probably all sorts of crews would pick you up."

"I'll be back, Sal."

"I won't stalk you like Brooke, and she'd give you whatever you wanted. But I can't, and I have my own dreams."

"Sal." I reach out and place my hand on hers. Our

fingers intertwine. "I'll come back to you. And Sal, Mox knows. He knows what happened to Drew."

Her fingers tighten, and she nods. "I'll do it; I'll write about it." Without warning, she lets go of my hand and slides off the dock into the water. She resurfaces, and her eyes dance. "Do you know I need you?"

"I need you, too." I smile. "So how much do you like Scottie?" I ask.

"I like him."

"The same like as a pet, or what?"

"Not a pet. But if he was, he'd be a big dependable Saint Bernard that rescues people and has some sense."

I yank off my shirt, dive down into the water, surface ten feet from her big eyes. "Saint Bernard. Ever wanted a pit bull? You know, the ones that bite without warning and don't obey and terrify the neighbors?"

"I used to, and I thought I could get over that desire."

I swim a couple of feet away.

"How about you?" She splashes me. "You like leash types or wild types?"

"I'm confused about that."

"That's fair." She bites her lip. "What are you feeling right now?"

"Unsafe."

Salome smiles and submerges. I go after, and somewhere beneath the water, her body brushes mine, moonlight glints in her eyes, and we dance—a beautiful submerged dance full of touch and light. I don't want air. I no longer need it, but after a minute, Salome must and breaks toward the surface. I turn a somersault and follow.

We swim toward the boat.

It's Salome, my ultimate rush, who I want.

It's time to destroy the Rush Club.

CHAPTER 28

THE NEXT AFTERNOON I HELP Troy move essentials from his house to the villa. He'll spend days with the crew during fire season. Cheyenne doesn't speak to me, but she peers at me as if I know something she doesn't. It's disconcerting, so I smile and nod and scurry each load out to Troy's truck.

Troy doesn't speak much either. His something approaches, and it scares the wits out of him. Weeks ago, I would have thought him weak for being scared. Not now. Not since my swim with Salome. All I've known—the cloudy wall separating me from the world—is gone. In its place is fear. Fear in the morning and at night.

Fear I understand—because I finally have something to lose.

THAT NIGHT I FIGHT SLEEP, the battle raging as furious as a wildfire blaze. Hours pass and I can't take it and slip into the living room. Troy is face to carpet.

"What are ya doing?" I ask.

He looks up slowly, his cheeks red and sweaty. "Do you pray, Jake? Do you ever pray or anything?"

"No. The thought of being watched all the time freaks me out. Figure if I don't talk to Him, I'll slip under the radar."

"But you do think there's a Him up there."

"Salome does."

I stare down at him, and he drops his gaze.

"I'm scared, Jake," he says.

"Me, too."

Troy pounds the floor.

"Tell me what you gotta do," I say.

"What time is it?"

"One thirty A.M."

Troy stands, puts on his jacket—the Immortals one—and slaps my shoulder. "Live short and loud, right?"

He quietly steps toward the entryway, turns the knob, and leaves the villa.

I stare at the closed door and listen to my ears ring. I don't remember this feeling before, and can't name it now, but it's close to cowardice. And the urge awakens, like it used to months ago, not the need, but the *urge*. I want to do whatever Troy's doing and risk whatever he's risking.

I throw on my clothes and set out after my friend. It's silent in the compound—fighting a fiery beast does that to guys trying to catch a few hours of sleep. I round our villa and pop onto Winders Street. Four shadows stand in the distance.

"Hey!" I holler. "Wait up."

All face me, and I start down the middle of the street—first slowly, then faster and faster until I'm nearly in a jog. Three shadows—Troy, a chubby one, and his friend—jog in the other direction, but the fourth one strides straight for me. We take the same line, and as his face comes visible, it's fierce.

"Stop, Jake," Mox orders.

I pick up my speed. I'll lose Troy.

"I said let it go," he hollers.

I break for the curb, so does Mox, now a bullet that fires straight for me. He lunges at my legs, but I cut back, and Mox sprawls onto the grass. I race after my friend.

"I know where she lives," Mox calls.

Mox's voice is weak, barely audible over the pounding of my boots, but it stops me, chills me, spins me.

He slowly rises, brushes off his jacket.

"The turret room. I know where she lives." He turns his back on me and vanishes into the dark of the night.

My head swivels from Troy to Mox. Feet stick where they're planted. He wouldn't do anything to Salome.

I jerk legs forward and turn the bend behind Troy. Fatty and Fez are big, they won't move fast.

I pound around the corner and pull up. Ahead, the three hop into Fatty's Jeep and speed down Dowling.

Dowling dead-ends. There's nothing beyond it. Nothing but the Spires. Crap.

I break toward Dad's, and five minutes later I pound his door.

Inside, a light flickers, and I hear a shuffle, a curse, then the door opens. Dad's face turns white. "What's wrong? Come on in." He reaches for my arm, but I pull it away.

"I need your truck. Can I borrow—"

He disappears for a moment, returns, and jams the keys into my hands. "You're not in any trouble? This isn't about you, is it?"

"No. Thanks." I race toward the truck.

Moments later, I squeal onto Dowling, where the thump of tar morphs to gravel's crunch. Stones plink and ricochet off the Ford's underbelly, and I slow, turn off the lights, and descend. I've walked this road a hundred times, but never driven it—the Beetle would never have made it. Winding deep down into one of the many canyons framing Brockton, the road is the only way in or out of our main tourist attraction: the Spires.

A half hour later, I reach them—enormous, jutting swords of rock that thrust one hundred feet out of the canyon bottom. Gray and angular, the fifty spires are razor sharp at the peak.

At least they were the last time I climbed one.

I'm alone here. It makes no sense. The road leads nowhere else.

Voices. From up above.

I strain my gaze, and against the moonlight I see shifting and wings. A hang glider. Some fool strapped in. Some fool named Troy.

If he flies down here, he'll be carved to shreds.

I grab the flashlight from the glove compartment, jump out of the truck, and weave between the spires. I race away from the cliff on which Troy stands. Toward the knoll I know well—the only one where you could land a glider before you crashed into the opposite cliff.

Breath quickens. Thighs burn.

Wait, Troy. Stall.

Hard earth turns to weed and finally grass beneath my feet, and I double over to catch my breath. I peek up.

Troy pushes off.

His glider catches no air and the wings totter side to side.

"Fight it! Pull hard!" I shout, but he can't hear. An updraft catches his glider and lifts him high before it releases him and he plummets toward rocky needles.

I flash my light over and over. Wave it above my head. He straightens the glider, skims the top of the spires, and angles down, straight for me. I drop my light and leap out of the way.

Troy hits hard, his glider cracks, and he tumbles wing over wing. I peek toward the cliff. Fez and Fatty stare down. They can't see me, not yet. I duck into a spire shadow and crawl toward my friend. He groans, and coughs, and starts to laugh. It's a weak laugh, but a laugh just the same. He'll make it. He's okay.

"That was the worst landing I've ever seen." I start to unstrap him.

"What are you doing? Get out of here," he whispers. "I'm not doing another one of these. They can't know you helped. Go!"

I slink back to the truck, wait for the watchers to vanish, and slowly creep up the hill.

The rush. This isn't a game.

I WAKE THAT MORNING TO Troy's war dance. His face is puffy, one arm's in a sling, and his right knee is wrapped. But he leaps and bounds on the bed, jumps off it.

"Looks like you're, uh, just fine," I say, and push up to an elbow.

"Better than fine. Initiation over. Cheyenne gets her wish. I get mine."

"Okay, I'm happy for you." I swing my feet over.

He jumps on my bed, leaps up, bangs his head, and laughs. "Feels so good."

"You're crazy."

He exhales, "Maybe." Troy coughs hard. "But what was really crazy was that little light. If I hadn't seen that light, I would've hit— Well, I would've been done." He steps off my bed and winces. "I tell you, that might have been my first serious prayer. That's probably why God sent me this funny-looking angel."

I rub my hand through my hair. No halo.

"Glad to help."

His voice lowers. "And Mox told me—your spin comes tonight."

"Tonight."

"I wouldn't worry. There's nothing on that wheel that you haven't already done. This should be no problem."

I rub the carpet with my feet and feel a shock. That was before fear crept in and took up residence. That was before Salome brought fire to my heart. Then it didn't matter, these stunts didn't matter.

I touch my face the way Salome did underwater.

Now life counts.

CHAPTER 29

MY SPIN COMES TONIGHT.

I spend the afternoon at the train depot, swinging my legs out of a boxcar and talking to Salome on my cell. The old "us" has returned, and the words fall free. I joke and she laughs, and spaces of quiet feel like home. But toward evening, our conversation turns heavy, and I can feel her fear.

The 8:10 rumbles by, and Salome falls silent.

"I need to go," I say.

"Are we going to be okay?" she says. "You could go to your dad's right now and borrow his truck and leave and—"

"He knows where you live. We can do this." I pause. "I guarantee it."

DARKNESS FALLS, AND I wander back to the villa. I open my door and stare at twenty men in jackets. They have the look I know well, the insatiable glimmer of a monster that needs to be fed. My shoulders droop. My monster is gone, and I'm alone.

"It's your night." Mox smiles evil. "Are you ready, friend?"

"Let's get this over with."

We march quietly down the path toward the clearing. I look around. Everyone seems confused. Except me. For the first time I'm crystal clear on pretty much everything.

I push by Troy and grab Mox's sleeve.

"All that ceremony takes a long time." I pat his back. "Are you all right if we skip that and jump to the spinning?"

He stops. I stop. He starts, and I quickly catch up.

"This isn't *Wheel of Fortune*," he hisses. "This isn't a game."

"What is it, then?"

Twenty minutes later, we trundle into the clearing. It takes twenty more to get in position around the post that will soon support my destiny wheel. The Immortals speak as if they're in church, as if this is a take-off-your-shoes moment. Theo from the hand crew lays his hand on my shoulder. From across the fire, Brian from Dozer #2 shakes his head. I don't need their sympathy, and I glance at Mox. He speaks and people nod, but his voice garbles.

"Jake!" Mox backhands my chest.

"Sorry, not paying attention, what's up?"

He seethes, and it hits. This is his moment. His most fearsome moment. It's strange not to care right now. Bet that pisses him off.

From the corner, a laugh. Mox walks toward it, whispers. It silences.

"Bring out the wheel!"

The big wooden disc comes out, and I stare down. Made from the gigantic side to a spool of cable, the wheel looks old and rickety, not terrifying. I get the feeling it would apologize, if it could, for how it's being used. Hunks of wood that could be its twin are in my mom's sculptures. Except for the names. This wheel is covered with them, charred by a soldering iron into the pine. My gaze zeroes in on two.

Kyle Ramirez. Andrew Lee.

An awkward wooden hand on top completes the deal

and bounces independent of the wheel itself.

I take a picture with my mind, one I can give to Salome. I wonder what she's doing right now.

From the left, a chant begins. "Spin, spin—"

I reach down and spin. The night quiets. The men quiet. The wheel wobbles to a stop. "Waterfall dive. Nighttime." I say. "Which waterfall, Mox?"

"Chisel Falls," he announces.

"Okay. So, tonight? Tomorrow? I'd just as soon be in the spin as brief a time as possible, 'cause I got something I need to do."

Mox tongues the inside of his cheek and leans toward me. His breath heats up my ear. "Nobody mocks me."

He reaches into his pocket and pulls out a compass. The men murmur, all except for Troy. He squints at the tiny object in Mox's hand. Troy has rotten vision. It's amazing he even saw my flashlight beam.

"What is that?" Troy blurts.

Mox shoves him away and approaches me.

"Spin again, Jake."

I squint at the dial. "What's on this one?"

"You stole Koss from me. It's time you understand how it feels to watch someone you care for risk everything for nothing." He holds out the spinner. "Spin."

I reach up and flick the plastic spinner, hear it whiz and come to an abrupt halt. Fez digs out a flashlight, lights up Mox's hand. The tiny metal spinner is divided into only two sections, each marked by one word. One name, Scottie. The other, Salome.

My arrow points at Salome.

"If you want to be a member of the Rush Club, she has to make the jump with you."

My heart pounds. Knees weaken, and I step back, bump into a body, and stagger back farther.

"What is this? She can't do that."

"Whoa now—" Fatty looks at me, drops his gaze, and waggles his head.

"I've seen his file," Mox says. "There's nothing on this wheel that's new to him. The intensity must be equal for us all."

I glance around. Faces vanish into the night. Only Mox remains. I plop down.

"You rookie thief," Mox says. "Did you think I'd forget my years with Koss? And what do you care about Salome? Doesn't she belong to your brother?" His rasp sounds faint, but his outline fronts me.

You're sick.

I bend over, bury my head in my hands before looking up. "You care about the people you rescue. Why don't you care about the men who fight fire beside you? Take Troy, he's a rookie who'd do anything for you."

"The *men* I fight with are all that matters in this world." Mox stares off. "I'm doing the feds a favor. If they won't weed out the weak ones at the start, I will." He stares at me, eyes sad. "Before good men die."

I frown. "Did a good man die?"

"Die? No." Mox straightens. "He's immortal."

CHAPTER 30

MID-CAL STATE WAKES UP lazily on Saturday morning. Carefree kids with carefree faces whip Frisbees across the lawn. I could have been one of them. They have no problems, no real ones.

I pull up to Salome's castle.

The miles from Brockton to the university have sucked the courage out of me. Words I've practiced now jumble in a suddenly cloudy mind. I'd rather jump into a blaze than walk up to the steps.

I have no plan. I know of no way to convince Salome to join me on this stunt. I know only that, if I can, I'll protect her. I also know she won't jump. I won't let her. She'll come. That's all. With that big old camera. Because if she doesn't, it's my word against Mox's, and Brockton already has its opinions.

I reach for my cell. She doesn't answer hers. I reach down, grab a pebble, and whip it toward the turret. Wind steals my throw, and I grab a bigger stone, hurl it harder. Too hard. High above, a shattering.

Shoulders droop, and I stare at the sidewalk. I wait for Scottie's act-responsible speech, his grow-up speech. I'd rather be showered with glass than his words.

The front door creaks, and I close my eyes and brace. Arms wrap me, gentle arms squeeze a smile out of me. A smile so big and loopy I feel it.

"Where'd my brother slink off to?" I peel Salome away.

"I'm not sure." Salome smiles. I frown.

She hugs me again. "I'm not sure I care."

Peel number two. "I'm not sure I understand."

She smacks my shoulder. "If you push me away one more time—"

"Fine!"

We hug angry, and it feels right. Salome steps back and points up. "You broke my window."

"Yes, yes, I did."

"But you also came back to me."

She grabs my hand, and we walk across the street and onto the grassy expanse. "So this is the tough college life." I gesture around the campus.

Salome squeezes my hands and turns me in a slow circle. "It's a brutal existence. And how's Mox? How was the spin? I should get my notebook. I'm ready for the facts."

I don't speak.

"You're a tough interview today. I'll start." She squeezes harder. "Are you finished? Is the club finished? If you want me to write this up, I'll need more than a hand-shake."

"Not quite."

She shakes her head. "Scottie called to warn me. I'm supposed to stay away from you." A lazy smile spreads across her face. "Your brother's a smart guy. I love his sensible brain."

I stop. "So why are you here with me?"

She turns me and takes my other hand. "I love your sensitive heart."

"Oh, boy." I squint. "I might need a little more help from you than I thought. Here's the deal. Mox asked me to join the Rush Club and—"

"The Rush Club. Such a catchy headline. You said yes, go on."

"I said yes. Everyone has to do some crazy initiation stunt. I saw it. The wheel. The words." I point to my head. "All captured in my cloudy brain. There's a spin. There's a task. There's Mox." I swallow. She's never stared at me so intently. "I spun, and if I want in, there's a nighttime jump off Chisel Falls."

Salome's face is blank, then she breaks into a long exhale. "At least it landed on lunacy you've already done."

"Not with you, I haven't."

Salome straightens and squirms. "What do I have to do with—"

"I've done everything on that wheel. He said he needed to up the intensity. Your coming with would sure do that."

She frowns. She knows I'm holding back.

I puff out air. "He's got it in for me. He hates Dad and Scottie. He blames me for Koss. That's a lot of hate."

I pull her toward a bench, sit her down, and kneel in front.

Her tanned face whitens. "This is crazy. No. Forget it." Her brows furrow, and her voice softens. "You don't want me to do this."

"Nope. I don't. Just write this up like we planned,

only I need you to come and bring the camera. This club has survived countless investigations. As I spun, it hit me that I need art to seal the deal. I searched for that wheel when Mox left after my spin. Something that big you'd think I could find it, but it's nowhere."

It's quiet a long time.

"So you came back to ask me to jump off of a hundred-foot cliff."

I squint. "No. It'll look like it, but no. I just need you to drive with me to the jump." I lift my hands, palms up. "It's all I can think of. Then it's over."

"Mox has this much contempt for you?" She stands and runs one hand through her hair, paces back and forth.

"You won't even be near the top of the falls. You just take pictures and write about it afterward. Then we're done."

"We?"

I nod. "We."

"What have you stumbled across? It's a nightmare. He's a freakish nightmare."

"Do you trust me?" I ask.

She stares at me a long time. "With my life."

CHAPTER 31

THREE DAYS LATER, I DRIVE to Mid Cal at midnight, my ears hyperaware. Of the rhythmic clunk of road joints and of heavy breathing. Fez and Fatty ride in the back—spotters, I'm told.

"Say, Fez, tell me something." I turn, and the car swerves around the mountain pass. His face goes pale. "What's up with you and Mox? When he's around, you guys are mute."

"Watch it!" He lurches forward, grabs the wheel, and twists right. I squeeze his wrist until he releases.

"If you don't want to come, fine," I say. "But keep the hand off the wheel."

Fatty chortles, and Fez drops back in his seat. "Pull over at Hanburg's. I need a drink."

I ease into the liquor store parking lot, and Fez hops out.

It's cold tonight. Midday heat has given way to a chill I haven't felt all summer. I shiver inside, and turn our plans over in my mind looking for cracks.

Fatty sits quietly in the back.

"Don't judge Moxie too soon," Fatty says. "All you see in him is this monster, this crazy. In your place, I don't blame you. But you don't see the man who saved us more times than we can count."

I turn and face him square. "So why this?"

He peeks up and glances at the liquor store.

"About twenty years ago, three best friends joined an elite smoke-jumping crew in Oregon. No zip lines, just a leap into a blaze's waiting arms. But they were crazy. Immortal, they thought." Fatty breathes deep and smiles. It's a gentle smile—one that doesn't fit his face. "A fire went worst-case scenario. Four men jumped. Mox and Koss were paired. Kip, the third, drew a rookie who was on his first live jump. They fell beneath the smoke canopy. Mox has never told me what happened next." Fatty's eyes sharpen, and his shoulders droop. "Kip's partner, that rookie, well, even with all that training, his body

RUSH

gave out. He couldn't keep up with Kip, and Kip per-
ished. Mox's other half died, and Mox never recovered.
He and Koss left the smokers, wandered around, and
five years later ended up joining the feds here in California."

Fatty stares into the liquor store. I peek, too. Fez
walks toward the register.

"Finish it," I whisper.

"The Forest Circus takes almost anybody. Oh, they
post stringent physical recs, but the truth is, you can
fail the tests and still they'll take you. It happens all the
time." He pauses. "Look at me.

"But Mox and Koss decided if the feds weren't going to enforce recs, they'd find a way to weed out weak
minds and bodies before they got to the line and got
another Kip killed."

I exhale slow. "The Rush Club."

Fatty tightens his lips. "If you live through it, you can
live through anything, and like Kip's memory—"

"You're immortal."

He nods, looks off. "Let's hope Salome is." His breath
gets heavier. "It seems cruel, but he's just doing what
the feds won't. Can you see that?"

Fez hops back in, still muttering.

Fatty's right about one thing: I don't know Mox at

all. We drive to Salome's in silence. I ease off the road and honk three times. Salome pushes into the night and strolls toward the Jeep. She glances toward the back, and her gait slows to a shuffle.

I push her door open. She keeps her gaze fixed on me. "No Beetle? I guess it would have been tight for the henchmen."

"Yeah," I say.

We drive into the mountains toward Chisel's Peak. I reach my hand toward Salome, and she takes it, cradles it in her lap. We're one jump from freedom, and I stroke her hand with mine.

The sound of water deep and strong, like a distant thunder, grows louder with each wind of the road. My mind is so clear, so focused. The dead feeling I've lived with forever is so far from me that I smile. I peek at Salome. She bites her lip and prays.

The Jeep rounds a bend, and I pull into a scenic turnoff. Beneath a half-moon, the hundred-foot waterfall crashes foam into the pool below. I know Chisel, know just how to jump it.

"You'll watch from here?" I turn and ask.

Fez nods. "Good luck."

Fatty gets out, opens the door for Salome. I peek over and watch him scuff the ground. "This ain't right," he says. "This goes too far. Bringing you in is wrong—"

"Fatty!" Fez hops out, rounds the Jeep.

"You want to tell me what she's got to do with the club? With Kip? With quality control? This ain't on my hands." Fatty looks at me, back to Salome. "I'll say you both did it. You don't need to do this, Salome."

Fez grabs his buddy and shakes. "What's gotten into you?"

"Will you two look over here?" I grab Salome's camera from the seat and flash the night.

"What's that for?" Fez blinks.

"I want to remember the event. Salome?"

She gives Fatty a hug. The big fella stares at his hands like he's never had one before. He finally hugs her back.

Salome releases, smiles, and walks over to Fez. The slimeball stretches out his arms, and she kicks him in the kneecap. He starts a wild hop.

"Get in the Jeep, Fatty!" Fez winces and curses, and the big guy obeys. Fez hands us each a flashlight and massages his leg. "So both of you flash us at the same time. Be sure you're a distance apart, then we'll know you're both up there. After the dive, we'll pick you up at the bottom."

Together, Salome and I set off into the night.

We snake the footpath, the wild crash of water strengthening with each step. I take her hand. "We've done a lot of crazy things together."

"You've done a lot of crazy things."

"Are you okay?"

"No."

I stop.

"But let's get this story on the fire chief's desk and then in *The Mid-Cal Reporter*, page one." She pulls me along.

The path cuts the pine forest, and we descend slowly to the river that falls off the edge of the world. Chisel Falls.

Ripples on the Chisel River glint and dance. They bubble into waves, then tiny breakers, golden in the moonlight. Then they disappear. It's where I'll disappear.

"I can't get much closer to the edge." Salome stares at the drop a hundred feet from where we stand.

"You don't need to. Stay here. I'll head to the edge. Watch for my signal." I gaze back toward the observation area. "From their angle, it will look like you're right up close."

I run along the bank, stand on my launching rock, and spin. I raise my hand, Salome does, too, and we flash our lights. I race back. "Now we need to move fast. The path I showed you yesterday? Take it down to the sitting rock behind the falls. Take pictures all the way. Here"—I take off my jacket—"get a good shot of this, of me now.

"It's so loud," I continue, I don't think you'll hear me hit water. But I'll flash you once with the light right before I dive. It's a tough swim beneath, so don't worry. It'll be a minute until I surface."

Salome presses against me. "I don't know if I should be proud of you, or hate you or . . ."

"Or?"

Salome kisses my cheek. "For luck."

I tingle and stroke her head. "You don't believe in luck."

"You're right." She kisses the other cheek. "For me."

"We need to get you down there before they get there. Stick to the trail. Go."

Salome vanishes. If she captures it all on film, the world will be right. Everyone will believe Scottie. No more kids will die trying to join the Rush Club. Then I'll finally tell Salome what I know—she's all the rush I need.

I scamper to my rock, strip to my trunks, and shiver. Spray coats the slippery rock. Now my job. It's not so tough, really—spring hard and I'll clear the falls. It's my takeoff angle. If I mess that up, I miss the pool below.

I swam it again yesterday to be sure. The deep pool holds plenty of rocks on the near side. As long as my feet don't slip when I jump, it's a piece of cake.

She should be there. I grab my light, shield the beam, and flash it once. Jump, splash, surface, then grab her and pull her in. We'll swim around the falls, get the camera, and leave. Mox's game will be over.

I stand, breathe deep, and jump.

It isn't real, not at first. Deep inside the mind, I expect to be caught, snatched back, like at an amusement park. But ten feet down the rush overpowers, and I wonder if this is what death feels like. A terrifying nothing. Not for just an instant, but long enough to be a new condition. It's a lifetime of acceleration and freedom and cold. I'm cold. Every part of me. Even my eyelids are cold—stuck open, seeing nothing. I glance down. More nothing. I've lost count. My entry count. There's no way to gauge it. I double over into pike position, lock frozen fingers together, and pinch my feet.

And open up too soon. I'm in position too soon, and I lose vertical. I brace. I need the water now. I need to hit now, or I'll land on my back and—

Smack! My shoulders and upper back strike water,

and I plunge deep. I bring half a breath with me. It's enough. My hands skim the river's pebbly bottom, and I place my feet, power toward air and life and Salome. And propel backward. Undertow surges against my chest. It steals oxygen and upward motion and pins me against rock. Weighty water crashes down, twists, and holds me tight. Air is gone, and I go limp, gulp water.

I'll die.

Salome's still waiting.

I bend into the flow, and the undertow squirts me away from the rock wall. I kick up, I think, and pop out fifty strokes from the falls. Sputtering and coughing, I reach for the shore and haul up. It's been seconds, or minutes.

Salome!

I stumble, vomit, and stumble on toward the falls, toward the ledge.

I see her, standing and shouting into the water.

"Jake! Can you hear me? Jake!"

"I'm—okay, I'm—" I cough, but the falls' crash devours my sputter.

"Are you there?" she screams, and I see her gray form dive straight down into the swirl.

"No!" I stagger around the falls to the ledge. I drop onto the bank beneath, wade in, and scream. Her hair whooshes gently around my knees. I reach down, see the gash where her head struck rock, and press hard against it.

"Help!" I stand and scream and stare at the limp girl in my arms.

CHAPTER 32

OUTSIDE THE HOSPITAL ROOM, nurses laugh. Their lives are smooth and full of hope. They will hop on elevators, throw off pastel uniforms, and forget her. But I will stay in this room. I won't move. I have nowhere else to go.

I'll sit here until she wakes.

I have so much to tell her—but I need her to come back. Wherever Salome is, I need her back, and I promise she'll always get the truth. Because now I can't hold it in.

Grim faces no longer scurry like rats, rush to every beep. She's stable. Their machines keep her alive.

They say Salome won't wake up, that she can't.

But they don't know her. Not like me.

I stare at my brother's face, cold and lifeless. There is nothing left of Scottie. My hands fold, and I count the freckles on floor tiles.

I rise and walk to the bedside table, reach through the tangle of IV drips, and finger the book, the tattered book. It's a Bible. Shouldn't be hard to open, but it is. I flip through. The words are small and many, and I wouldn't know where to start, though she'd want me to. I carry it to my seat and collapse.

And listen. The low hum from the vent, pushing the air that inflates Salome's lungs; the steady beep from a monitor near the bed; and a clock—a cheap wall clock. Its tick grows louder, pounds in my head.

Again tears fall, like they do every hour. I can't take this room, can't take that clock.

I stand and rip it off the wall, hurl it to the floor. Glass shatters. My brother doesn't flinch. I plop into the chair, throw the Bible onto broken glass, and lift the clock. I set my pointer against the hour hand. I turn back time. Three hours. Seven.

"What are you doing?" A nurse stands in the door. "You can't—"

One day, now another hour.

"Can you hear me, Jake?"

Two days, three days. Four. I stop. 1:00 A.M. I stare at the dead clock that jerks in rhythmic seconds against my finger. It tries to live. Four days ago, I did, too.

I stare at the nurse, old and thick, through swollen eyes.

"I did it all," I whisper.

"Things fall, accidents happen." She tiptoes toward me, lays her hand on my shoulder. "We'll get housekeeping." The nurse turns to leave, stops when she sees the Bible. "This shouldn't be on the floor."

She picks up the book, lays it on the nightstand.

I listen to the machines, grind shards into the floor with my boot, slump down, and close my eyes.

"Jake? Scottie?"

We both jump to our feet. Mrs. Lee stands in the doorway.

The nurse smiles. "I'll see to this mess. Be careful, Carol. An accident happened over there."

"An accident is still standing over there," Scottie mutters, does not look my way.

Mrs. Lee walks between Scottie and me, straight toward her daughter, the one I did in. She strokes Salome's hair, kisses her forehead, and whispers.

"Hello, darling. I'm back. The Kings were kind

enough to let me sleep a bit." She winks at me, turns, and likely does the same toward Scottie. "They're both such nice boys. You're very fortunate."

Fortunate?

I peek at Scottie. He cries again. I can't take it. All the niceness. Yell or curse or shout, but don't kill me with this niceness I don't deserve.

"I—I need to leave."

Neither turns their head. Mrs. Lee strokes. Scottie seethes.

"Maybe I'll come back tomorrow?"

"Don't bother." Scottie's jaw tightens, and muscles in his face twitch.

Mrs. Lee straightens and smiles. "That would be nice." She walks toward me, tiptoes through the glass. "You are so special to her. She needs you here."

I nod and bury my face in my hands. I feel a hand gently pull my fingers down. Mrs. Lee reaches into her purse and pulls out a small journal. Salome's journal. I'd know it anywhere.

"Here." She presses it into my hand.

I swallow hard. "Why give it to me?"

Mrs. Lee smiles. "This one's all about you. Cover to cover."

"Things have changed," Scottie hisses, leans over

Salome. He picks up a hand and kisses it.

"Maybe." Mrs. Lee's gaze stays locked on me. "Time will tell. Come back tomorrow, Jake."

I squeeze Salome's book and step out past the house-keeper in the doorway.

I drive into Brockton. There is nothing left here for me. My solve-it-all plan ruined everything. I pass Dad's place, the home he wanted me to visit. The bushes are overgrown; the lawn's unmowed. A week of flyers stuff the mailbox. Dad's dead. I killed him, too. I could have outed the Rush Club from the outside, he'd say. I should have listened to him, he'd say. I know what he's doing—he sits on the couch, knowing his son de-stroyed his town.

I glance back at the Lees', quiet and sad. Wreaths lean against the door. There is no place for me to lay my head. The villa is closed pending investigation. My interviews after that black night, Salome's photographs, and the sweet life I destroyed see to that. Firefighters, heroes in this world, hate me, too.

Mox is suspended. To the town, an icon has fallen—chopped down too soon. It doesn't know why; it feels no relief that other fighters are safe. All Brockton knows is that a Jake King stunt put Salome in the hospital.

I drive up the mountain, to the only place I know I'm

welcome. I sit among the junk with Salome's journal.

Hour after hour. I forget why I'm there there, remember, and forget again. I think about fifth grade and Mom's salmon dinners and the journal I don't dare open. I remember my first home run and Dad's whoop, my last home run and his empty seat on the bleachers. Night falls, and I still sit.

I lose strength, let my body fall. Alone, I cry.

CHAPTER 33

I WAKE, STAND UP IN the heat of morning, and hop on the dirt bike.

I race laps around my jump, tire of the view, and turn into the trees. Away from Brockton. Up the mountain. I've never been here before. I ride hard and straight and can't shake her sheet-white face from my mind.

Soon thighs burn, the engine scalding me through denim.

I break free into a clearing and throw down my bike. Sweat stings my eyes, and I swipe beads away with a soaked T-shirt. I squint forward. Trees stretch on forever.

I owed Koss. Now I owe Salome.

I turn around, stare back down. The wind blows hot, scorches my already hot cheeks.

What would she want? What do I want?

Jake, come back to me.

I race down toward the salvage yard. Faster I fly. Trees blur by me.

Slow down.

The voice is small, but real. I ease on the throttle.

Slower still.

I reach my jump, rev the engine, and power up the takeoff ramp.

Stop.

I do.

I look down over the twisted metal. Ahead, there is weightlessness and everything I've known.

I glance at hands covered with Salome's blood. And I think. All is still. My mind is at rest. All urges are gone— the monster's grip doesn't hold.

I let the bike roll back down to solid earth.

From here, I see clearly. I feel it all. I am free, free to stay with the one I love.

I walk my dirt bike to the road, hoist it high, and strap it on top of the Beetle. Won't need it up there anymore. I wind down to Dad's.

Once there, I stand on the step and pound. I've pounded for minutes. The man's in there. I kick the door with my boot, and it slowly opens.

What the—

There is little left of the dad I grew up with, the man I spoke with days ago. Vacant eyes, slumped shoulders. He looks at me, I think. It's hard to tell if he sees.

"Do you mind if I drop off my bike? It needs work. I thought maybe I could spend time in your garage and—"

"I've been waiting for you," he whispers.

It's the one response I'm not ready for, and I run hands through my hair and nod. Dad turns, leaves the door open behind him, and vanishes. I unstrap the dirt bike and follow close behind.

I walk into the dining room and stop. The house is a dump. But there's no junk. Old trunks full of Mom's pictures and letters, report cards of mine and Scottie's. His old blankie, my stuffed animals.

"I was just . . . going through some things. Your mom's. Both of you boys'."

I walk around, pick up pictures of Scottie and me. Our family and the Lees. Salome and me holding hands when we were three.

I hold it up. "Can I keep—"

Dad smiles. "Yeah."

I nod. "I just stopped in to say I know I made a mess of things. That accident was totally my fault. I can't blame it anyone else. I thought it through. I mean, Salome agreed to it." I blink. "No. She agreed to *me*."

He inhales slow. "I want you home. Both of you boys. It's the right place, you know."

"It's probably not going to happen. Scottie isn't talking to me, unless it's under his breath. But the offer is great."

Dad nods. "How about you, then? I don't know where you've been these days since the accident, but I'd sure love to have you around." He pauses, forces a smile. "I don't know that I can shut Brockton up. I can't fire everybody." He smirks. "This town can be brutal. But if anyone can take it, I figure it's you."

"Yeah," I whisper. "I'll stay. Least for now." I walk to the window. Outside it's calm, but dark. Too dark for daytime. "What's the word out there?"

"That you hurt Salome to get back at Scottie. That asshole Mox spread that one right up until his suspension, right up until he disappeared." He shakes his head.

"And the guys? Where'd they all end up?"

"Most Brockton bucks are staying with their parents,

and a bunch of folk are putting up the out-of-towners, just until the investigation's over and things get back to normal." He joins me at the window. We rub shoulders and stare at nothing, at least I don't.

"So this club. Everything Scottie tried to tell me was true?"

"Everything Scottie said was true." I open the window, sniff, and look at Dad.

"The Grasston blaze. If we had wind, she'd be on our doorstep. They'll knock it down. It's eighty percent contained. You haven't been following it?"

"Time does funny things sitting in a hospital room. I'm heading back there." I hold up the yellowed photo. "Thanks for the picture." I shuffle toward the door.

"Say hello to Carol and Jacob for me," Dad says.

If Scottie lets me.

CHAPTER 34

CLOUDS ROLL IN. NO RAIN.

I know I should get to the hospital, but I plunk onto the steps in my house and turn the journal over in my hands. Maybe I am the star of the show, but Salome never offered me a peek; in fact, she slammed it shut more times than I remember. I'm more frightened than eager to read it. I know how each entry will sound to my ears.

What were you thinking, idiot? Say how you feel.

I stand and press the journal against my nose. Her scent is gone, there is only the pine-tinged sweetness of smoke. Inside, I start to tingle.

I walk out to my car as the Lees' garage door rises. *Crap.*

"Jake?"

No way can I look him in the eyes. I slip my hands and the journal behind my back, then kick the ground. "Mr. Lee."

He jogs over and gives me a hug I don't know what to do with. "Heading to see Salome?"

I nod. He must catch a view of the journal, and he pulls my arm in front of me. We both look at her words in my hands.

"She loves to write."

"Always," I say.

Mr. Lee looks up, closes his eyes, and groans. It's a frustrated groan.

"Got room for me?" he asks.

No. I have absolutely no room for you.

"Yeah," I say.

He closes his garage door, rejoins me by my car. "I'm glad we get some time alone."

I risk a peek at his face. His wrinkles are deeper, but they hold no rage. They still mark him only when he smiles. But those eyes, they sear with something new. Determination, I guess. They've always been tough to look at—now it's darn near impossible.

A hot gust carries the smell of a burn, and light flakes whisk between us. We both look up.

"Can you see that?" he says. "It's getting closer."

"There's not enough wind. Tonight, I bet the clouds will open up." I force a smile. The smell ignites dry tinder inside me, and my body grows tense.

"The radio is talking possible evacuation." He hops in the car. "They've already lost twelve homes in Grasston."

"That's a ways off. Clearing Brockton would be paranoia."

We pull out. Mr. Lee sets his hand on the journal that rests between us.

"Have you had a chance to read this yet, Jake?"

I wonder what to say, what to hold. "No," I lie. "I mean, I can't . . . open it." My leg bounces against the Volkswagen wheel. "More paranoia."

In the distance, a siren sounds. The wicked one. Firefighters up. Brockton's crews get ready for dispatch, wherever you are. Men, women, the feds need all hands on this blaze.

But inside me, all is quiet; I'm drawn to a different emergency.

The hospital in Chisel Falls is half an hour from Grasston—not far enough. I peek at Mr. Lee. He nods.

"Floor it."

AT THE HOSPITAL, ORDERLIES and nurses talk quick and quiet and flash nervous smiles. They don't fool a soul. It's California. It's the season, and even these vented halls fill with the scent I know so well.

Scottie is still there. He reads a book to Salome. I think he'll make a mighty good husband, to somebody else.

"Hey, Scottie," I say.

"Mr. Lee." Scottie rises, goes and pats Jacob on the back.

I walk toward the bed, lean over, and whisper to Salome. "If you come over again, I promise I'll beat him to the door."

"Guys."

I know the voice, and my gut twists. The voice isn't here; it can't be. I slowly peek over my shoulder, straighten, and face it.

Scottie grabs a chair to steady himself. His knuckles redden, then whiten, then stretch and fist, and soon Salome won't be the only one lying down. Mox shifts his weight and fiddles with the hat in front of him.

He can't be here. There's no way.

"We've been called. Everybody's been recalled. Active, suspended. It's comin' this way via Brockton.

There are high winds and hot spots all around us, and they're throwing the world at it."

Scottie rushes at him, grabs him by the jacket, and pins him against the door frame. Mox is limp, a rag doll. "See her? Do you see what you did?" He rears back.

Mr. Lee grabs his arm. "Let him go."

"He took Kyle and Drew. He took Salome. Don't you know who this is?"

Mr. Lee gentles Scottie away from Mox, turns, and stands in front of Mox's expressionless face. "Salome is my daughter. Do you bear any responsibility for her lying here?"

Mox shifts. "Yeah, I do."

Mr. Lee nods. "You're an honest man."

"No." Mox swallows. "I'm not."

Mr. Lee's gaze has him pegged.

"Do you know what it's like to see your daughter day after day, but not hear her voice. Not hear her say, 'I love you'?"

Mox looks down, his rasp barely a whisper. "No." Mox has disappeared, and this is the shell of a man I haven't met.

"You could lose your daughter if we can't stop this fire." Mox's eyes plead. Mr. Lee turns, and his gaze falls on Salome. He moves slowly toward her, bends over, and rests his forehead on hers. His words come barely audible.

"I know you hear all this. Don't worry, Jake won't let it near you."

I clear my throat, and Mr. Lee gazes up at me, before straightening, his voice clear and strong.

"Boys, bury it."

MOX, SCOTTIE, AND I SPEED toward Brockton. The air hangs hot and heavy and unnatural, and a series of charcoal plumes crested with orange rise from the horizon.

In the Jeep, sandwiched between two men who likely hate me, makes for a quiet ride.

We meet Fatty near the villa, gear up, and buddy-check en route to the airport and our waiting copter. Troy's already been dispatched, but along with Fez, we're five strong with three packs in tow.

Scottie's gaze fixes on me. He trained to rappel, but he's never done it live. He looks scared and angry, and I don't know how to help him—speak up or shut up. So I give him a tight-lipped nod. He can do this. For her, he can do it.

We reach the port and leap out. Fatty and Fez stare at Mox. The blaze in his eyes—the crazy look that pumps us up and tells us it's showtime—is gone. His feet drag over the tarmac, barely carrying him toward the sound of rotors.

He's always the IC, always in charge. But not now.

"I'm taking IC." I shove Mox into the copter. "Any problems with that?"

Silence.

Mox reaches me the radio. "It's your show, kid."

I grab it, glance around the copter at nervous eyes. "Dispatch, Helicopter Five Hotel X-ray."

The gravelly voice fights through the noise. "Incident number four-four-three in Township Sixty-seven North. Landmark Carver's Gorge."

"Five Hotel X-ray is off the ground with five souls on board and showing ten minutes out."

There is silence. More gravel from the radio, then Lorna from dispatch's voice resounds.

"Who is this? Mox?"

"Negative. Jake."

"You've got to be kidding."

Scottie turns toward the window. "Well, that was encouraging."

WE HAVE OUR ORDER. If all goes well, we'll set back fires three miles out of town, along the top rim of the gorge. If it jumps the gorge, game over. It's a fueled sprint to Chisel Falls, where Salome lies.

Mox gently knocks his head against the glass, Fez and Fats look lost, and Scottie mutters. What a team.

"Don't worry, Scottie." I scoot over beside him. "They're evacuating Salome right now. I'm sure of it. You saw the nurses—"

"This doesn't change what you did."

He's right. It changes nothing.

CHAPTER 35

I ZIP DOWN THE LINE toward the top of the gorge, the gang of four close behind. It is near. Very near. We land near the lip, establish the safety zone, and peer down into the crack.

Wood splinters and cracks, and I whip around.

A dozer. My best friend right now. The hulking machine crunches up, and Keith Garrison leaps out. The right side of his face is charred black.

"I cleared her back from the lip. She's hot." He kicks the dozer. "Baby almost melted."

Steam hisses from the machine. "Give her a rest," I say. "We'll cut 'er and light her back." I slap Mox's back, and he nods. His head swivels from side to side, that once-fierce gaze doesn't snag on anything.

"Snap out of it, Mox." I kick his boot. "No time. No time!"

We secure our packs, and the five of us grab chain-saws and dash toward the inferno, across the tram-pled path the dozer cleared. Scottie winces, pulls up when he reaches the standing brush line. "Here!" he shouts.

"Closer." Mox looks up. "No use here. Push her back."

"Here!" Scottie rips the cord on his saw, and it snarls to life. The boys glance at Mox, then to me.

"Follow Scottie."

Saws roar and chew branches and stumps and left-overs Keith's dozer missed.

"Lots of food here!" Mox slaps my back. "This won't do. She'll reach here and speed-run to the gorge."

"And then?"

He points to the other side, at Brockton's second dozer hauled in and waiting for the dozer crew on the far side. "Thirty feet from here to there. One gust and she'll jump."

"What would you do?"

A pinecone explodes at his feet. "Cut in another

hundred feet here. In its teeth." Mox points to the other side of the ravine. "Just to buy time for *that* dozer to clear."

I nod, pause. "You wanted to kill Salome."

"No."

"You thought I'd make her jump?"

"She did."

Around us, trees heat and blister. Mox stares at them. We're not so different, he and I. The adrenaline that surges through us, the love of the rush. We're not so different. We could be brothers. Friends. In some other life, where fires and family and good and evil didn't exist.

"Let's knock it out," I say.

His eyes narrow, and the gleam returns. The wild flash that terrifies and comforts transforms his face, and he smiles.

"Fats!" he yells.

From in front, a whoop goes up, and Fatty and Fez tramp toward us. "You're back!"

Mox scans. Each smoking log and firebomb, every wind shift and surge of heat—it all goes into his head, twists and rearranges like the sculptures do in mine. He blinks hard; the plan's made. "Where's Scottie?"

"He won't go any closer." Fats throws up his hands.

"The boy's falling back to the dozer, to the safety zone."

"Fair enough." I take a slosh of water. "Go! Go!" We race toward the blaze. Heat rises with each stomp nearer the devourer, and ground sparks fly.

"You're too close, Jake! Here, we cut its throat here." Mox points to the sky and chainsaw roar fills the air. Mox dances and curses. We're on the line, we're doing what we know best.

It's a strange poetry, and from the outside, it looks random. But to an Immortal, to any fighter on the inside, the beauty is inescapable. Odd to call an ax and a chainsaw beautiful, but when eight arms sweep and saw, each move in concert, and behind it all, the heat and fury of the blaze. Yeah, it's stinkin' beautiful.

The fire crackles and hisses. I hiss back.

"Stay away from Sal. I won't lose her again."

A fueled tree limb explodes, falls, and missiles down the hill. It zips by and catches Moxie square across the chest. Both feet fly up, and his body propels backward. Sparks rain down on Fez and Fatty. They scream and fall back and claw at their faces.

I stand alone for a moment, frozen in the heat. A shadowy outline glows orange around the edges, races toward me, shouts, "Jake!"

"I'm here, Scottie. I'm okay. Man down!"

Scottie's fear-strengthened arms grab me and yank me back. I throw them off. Mox groans.

"He's not worth it." Scottie's eyes are wild. "Let's go!"

"No." I race back to Mox, his body a combination of rough breath, blood, and wood splinters.

"Drew," he coughs. "He made it through that ropes course, did his spin. We flew in to pick him up, but it was dark, and we tangled him up on extraction. You can tell Salome . . . he was a good man." Mox winces and lets out a groan. "Go, kid."

"No!" I lean into the scorching trunk that has him pinned. It scalds through my jacket, and I scream. Another push. The tree limb shifts and rolls off. I reach down, hoist Mox over my shoulder, and stagger back to the dozer.

"Get everyone out of here." Mox's voice is weak. "Fats, Fez . . . Scottie." Mox is losing blood from somewhere. By the time I reach the dozer, it covers my jacket.

I lay him in the cab. "Take him down, Keith."

Keith gives a determined nod and revs the engine.

Wind gusts, and fires pop up around us. One strong blow, and she'll leap the gorge.

"They dropped us on the wrong side," I say to the three remaining.

"It'd take hours to walk around this canyon." Scottie pushes back his helmet, winces, and wipes sweat from his forehead.

I look toward the canyon lip. "Yeah, it would."

CHAPTER 36

I WALK TO THE EDGE of the gorge and lay gut to ground. I drop my helmet into the abyss. Five seconds. Ten seconds later, I think I hear a crack from the helmet hitting ground. Either way, our rope won't reach.

"I need to go get my helmet."

"Don't, Jake." Scottie tries to act all big brotherly, but that time's past, and the dozer on the other side needs to move. The second crew hasn't been dropped in yet.

I lower myself over the edge, give the openmouthed guys a wink, and disappear. "Go down with Mox! Now." I traverse the wall. I'm too heavy in my gear, and my toe is too big to find the nooks; if I make it, it's a miracle. Even I'll call it that. Rock climbing is worse down than up. It's a blind thing. You can't see the ledges, and bad holds feel like good ones through the steel on my boot's toe. I bounce on each footfall, test the strength.

Twenty-five feet down I rest, hug the rock, peek up. Scottie's on his stomach—his face peeks over the edge.

"Get going, idiot!" I yell.

"Not until you're down. Keith and the others left."

"So you're lying there with no way down?"

He doesn't answer.

I move speedily, I have to. My body loses precious strength I'll need for the climb up on the other side. I take risks, stop testing holds, and scamper. Thirty feet from the bottom I double-time, finish in minutes. I run to my helmet. It's cracked in two.

So much for that.

I race across the cut and climb. Past Dusty's ledge and the tree that now smolders. I place my mind on Salome and climb as if she waits on top. And freeze.

Seventy feet up, I glance down. I can't move.

I've never been afraid of heights and have never understood those who are. Seems so unreasonable. It's only space, the same space as if you look toward the sky, except you're on the other side. But it hits. Panic. Fingers claw.

"What's wrong?" Scottie yells. "Move. Move!"

"Can't." I slap my face against rock. "I'm too high up—"

"Of course you are. You're a freak of nature, but you're almost there! Geez, Jake, do you know how high up you are—"

"Shut up!" I whisper. "Please."

You've done this hundreds of times in hundreds of places. You climb and dive and . . .

I vomit onto the cliff, and another nauseous wave crashes over me. Hands tremble, legs buckle, and in the cut all is still. But inside my head, this giant boulder swells, fills my mind. Thoughts fly off it like electric shocks, terrify me.

I'll never see her again.

"I want to live, Salome." I gather strength. "Live!" I holler. I hoist a shaking foot upward, bring it down on solid rock. I smile. It makes no sense, but I tingle with the thought of living. That thought is enough. *Snap.* My panicked fingers snap into action, and I wobble to the top, roll over the edge, and look back.

"I made it, Scott— No!"

Fire burns to the far lip. A wall of flames licks the
rim where my brother once lay. She broke through, ran
for the gorge, just like Mox said.

I cry and curse and flail toward the dozer. I climb
in, touch metal, and burn my flesh. "No!" I jam my
hands into my gloves and try again. The cab is a furnace. I turn the key, and she fires up.

"Now let's see what you got!"

I bulldoze angry. I'm no expert, but I know the prin-
ciple. The dozer senses my hate, takes it on, and
together we clear a swath back from the edge.

Hiss. All is steam, and for a moment I'm blind. I
look up, watch a copter rotor away for more water. It's
damp around me, and my heart soars. I turn to make
another swath, finish, and do it again. More water falls
on my world.

Then the wind gust comes. Sparks burst into my
cleared row. I watch. They fizzle, die out. Hours later,
I've made a third pass, then a fourth. It's night, and
hourly water drops push back the fire's reach. Wet.
Crunched. Beneath my line there's plenty of fire food.

The dozer chugs and quits. Out of gas.

I stagger from the cab, light-headed, fighting to stay
vertical.

Then I hear them.

Dull roars in the distance. With the dozer still, the sound of chainsaws cut through the ring in my ears. Crews battle on my left and right. I can't see them—I don't need to—but they're there. With me. I'm not fighting alone.

Two to one. Two hours work, one hour rest. Not tonight.

My heart swells. I grab the chainsaw from inside the cab, and it roars back to life. I will not leave my job. I will hold my line. Salome counts on me.

I work through the night, I think. Morning should come, but the sky is black. I work until my calluses bleed through my gloves, until my eyebrows singe into nothing, until I feel it—a breeze at my back.

She'll hold. With the wind shift, the line will hold. The flames across the gorge die down.

I collapse across a boulder, and my world spins. I must fall into sleep because I dream. I dream a voice calls to me over and over from across the abyss.

"You still there, brother?"

CHAPTER 37

I WAKE UP, STIFF AND SHORT of breath. I grab the water and tools from the dozer and start the long pack out. It's hours back to Brockton, but in the darkness of noon, it feels like days. The world feels emptier today. There's not so much to hate, not so much to love, either. How do I explain Scottie to Dad or Salome?

Or myself. Because I seem to have a hand in everything. Again, I was there, right there when Scottie died.

I told him to leave. He stayed on his own. To watch over me.

Tears fall easily. It's a loud, ugly cry, the kind I've seen in others, but worse. Because I don't cry well—don't know how to do it—and it croaks out in awkward bursts.

I choose the gentle roundabout way back, the one that splits the clearing of the Rush Club. The fire didn't get this close, and beneath the birdless darkness, flowers still bloom. I doubt the blaze is contained, but she's taken a few to the midsection. We'll likely stand.

In the murky day, the clearing where I spun the wheel feels foreign. The mystery, the club's strange attraction, has vanished with the sun. Now the grassy stretch looks like what it is: a place where countless young men made a decision to die.

"You should've burned." I glance at the fire pit. "If anything in this world should've burned, this place should have." I walk its perimeter and sniff. Ahead, there's a smoldering. It's partially me, covered with fire reek. But the scent strengthens. I walk into the bushes and freeze. A ring of dusty ground smokes.

I sweep earth away with my boot and stare at what lay beneath.

The Rush Club wheel is charred black.

I hoist it onto the grass, plop down beside it. "All to be in the spin. To be immortal."

The ground is dry, and I don't want to leave the wheel hot. I jam fingers beneath it and heft the disc onto its side. It balances, and I yank out my ax, rear back, and notice writing through my blurred gaze. On the back, left untouched by fire, carved into the wheel.

For tortured souls who have no home
Come and play
While you're young and free
Come and play
Before courage leaves and we die
Koss

I chop it into splinters. There will be no more game, no more playing.

Suddenly, the world spins. I turn from the pile and wonder if Kip knows what his death did, what his best friend did. I wonder if he sat and looked down and laughed or cried when Kyle died, when Drew died. I wonder what he'll say if he sees Mox again.

And inside my heart is a burning desire to read Salome's words, to find her and say hello. Would she hear a difference in my voice? Probably not. But I'll say it all the same.

BROCHTON IS A GHOST TOWN. Aside from the base manager, a few emergency vehicles, and exhausted crews sleeping in the villa, nobody's here. Keith crosses Main, and I give a shout.

He curses. "That can't be you, Jake."

"It's not."

He slaps my back, and I wince. "Let's get you to medical."

I gladly throw my arm around his shoulder and let him lead. For the next hours, I'm faceup in the medic's tent.

"Ninety percent contained, that's what they say." Aronson never could shut up. He sews up some spots, places cold sheets over burns. "Should be out of the woods here. Up mountain wasn't so lucky, but here we were, and sometimes that's all you can ask for, right?"

"Where exactly wasn't so lucky?"

"Oh, turns out there's an old junkyard up that face. It's a lost cause. Though a crew sure gave their all to save it."

I smile. It hurts. "I owe them for trying."

He nods. "Shouldn't be hard to thank them. It was Mox and your crew. Before they called you out, your whole team was up there fighting on their own. It's where

Troy was injured." He sets down his gauze. "Man was pinned beneath a collapsed ramp, but he'll be fine."

I lay my head back down. Life is so strange. Who to hate, who to love gets all jumbled in the living.

"Where's everyone now?" I ask.

Aronson shakes his head. "Mox was too bad off for my tent. We airlifted him to Chisel Falls."

"They didn't evacuate?"

"They didn't need to, I guess." He removes the cool squares from my skin. "It would've been tough. Some people there are pretty bad off." He looks at me, purses his lips. "But you already know that."

I rise slowly and drag over to Dad's. The key to the Beetle is buried beneath his heaps, but I find it, ease into the car, and zip toward Salome.

The hospital is full, every bed, a nurse says. In the hallways, zombie doctors whisk around gurneys and wheelchairs. You wouldn't know the worst was over.

I walk slowly through the chaos. A nurse ricochets off me and gasps. "Triage is first floor." She grabs what's left of my jacket. I gently remove her hand.

"I'm okay."

"Gwen!" A call from down the hall and she jumps, backs away slowly. "Stay right here. I'll have someone—take a look—"

"Gwen!"

She rushes away, and I continue toward the one door that matters more than any other.

I'm here. I'm not leaving again.

"The Rush Club did *your* job. Someone had to weed out the weak ones. Kip died because you didn't."

Mox?

I hear the voice and glance to my right. Mox is propped up, his face contorted. He still burns. Richardson and a man I don't know take notes from the other side of the bed.

The scene is too much. I've seen too much, lost too much.

Mox's gaze catches mine, and the others follow. I slump against the door frame.

Richardson stands. "Geez, Jake. Get yourself looked at."

I look at myself, boots to shoulders, and nod. I slowly slip out of my jacket, the one with the *I* ripped right down the middle. I toss it into the room.

"Doesn't fit anymore."

Mox squeezes his eyelids tight and winces. His lips part.

"Never did, kid."

I straighten and continue my shuffle.

"Do you want to explain that, Jake? Jake!" Richardson calls, but I've no desire to see the feds. Not today. Not tomorrow.

Salome is three rooms away.

Two. One.

I peek around her door frame and blink. Dad snores in a corner chair, the Lees hold hands and stare out the window, while Scottie leans over Salome and strokes her head.

He's alive!

He has his hand on Salome.

"Hey, brother." I say. Scottie flies at me, his face light and free. He checks me over and slugs my left rib. I groan.

He yanks me straight and hugs hard. Beyond him the Lees do the same.

"You weren't moving on the cliff, and that was a thousand gallons of water that fell from the heavy," Scottie whispers. "Not even you makes it through that."

"What about you?" I try to squeeze him back. "The whole rim burned."

"Not my survival tent. At least one of us actually uses that stuff."

I nod, peek over his shoulder "Anything new here?"

"All tubes are out." He releases me and turns toward the bed. "She's breathing on her own."

I push by him and lay my hand on Dad. He rouses, blinks, looks from Scottie to me. "Hey!"

He says more and hugs more, and the three of us feel like a three, but soon his words garble and the room fades, because there's somebody I haven't greeted yet.

I take Scottie's seat beside her.

Her face is perfect. Still. I know she knows. I know she hears.

"We took care of it. It's all done. Everything." I dig in my pocket and yank out a stone, blue and fiery. "I brought a bluey back from the hill for you. This is from our night, our almost night." I reach it onto the bedside table. "Wake up and we'll find more. I promise."

I glance over charred gear and close moist eyelids. Wake up, Salome. The nightmare's over.

There's no rush without you.

Behind me, a beep quickens, steadies, and my eyes open. Scottie walks to the bed, sits down at her feet. I lean back and exhale. It was just a beep. Just a strange—

Salome's eyes flutter open, and my body turns to lead. I can't stand. I watch her gaze flit around the room, skim the ceiling. It lowers, bounces off my brother three feet in front of her face, and makes for the window. Her gaze shifts and settles on me, and her little finger stretches toward mine.

"Jake."

Read an excerpt from
JONATHAN FRIESEN's moving novel

JERK,
california,

a *Schneider Family Book Award* winner

chapter one

"SAM HAS IT. QUESTION IS, HOW BAD?"

The pediatrician smiled. Like he got off on destroying a kid's life. Like children frequently went to sleep normal and woke up monsters who couldn't keep their damn bodies still.

He stared at me, waiting. My right hand twitched. He pointed and continued. "The disease has seasons. One day he'll flail like a windmill in spring. Then the wind'll die and you won't see anything for months." He turned to my mom. "There are some experimental drugs—"

"Who the hell is supposed to pay for those?" my stepdad said.

The doctor rose. "I can see you need some time, Bill." He shook my six-year-old hand, gave my stepdad a pat on the back, and slipped out of the examining room, leaving the three of us to stare at my jerking hands and shoulders.

"What'd he say, Mom? Bill? When's it gonna go away?"

Bill stood and paced the room. "Go away? Your twitches won't ever stop." He cursed and kicked the doctor's swivel chair.

I stared at Mom. "Never? Not even when I'm older?"

Mom scooted her chair in front of mine. "He says you have Tourette's."

I mouthed the word, and she leaned forward and stroked my arms. Gentle at first, then harder and harder and mixed with tears. I knew she was trying to rub that bad word out of me.

"What does that mean?" I asked.

"It means," Bill said, "you can forget about ever running my machines."

My hands squeezed the jacket Bill gave me, the green one with Tar-Boy on the front and a cement mixer on the back. I pulled free of Mom and grabbed Bill's pant leg.

"I can stop it. Please, Bill." I started to cry. "I'll be still. Promise!"

Old Bill turned his back, Mom closed her eyes, and even at six years old I knew I was alone.

chapter two

"YOU'RE QUIET IN GROUP TODAY."

Leslie, the social worker, stares at me. I look around at the others. Eight guys rest their heads on the table.

"Everyone's quiet," I say.

She places her young elbows on the table and rests her young head in her young hands. "But you're somewhere else, aren't you, Sam?"

Bryan snores from across the circle, and I point at him, but this woman's eyes won't go away. I glance at the clock—ten more minutes.

"I *wish* I were somewhere else. How many more weeks do I have to come?"

Dumb question. I know exactly. Ten. In Old Bill's barn hang fourteen sheets of paper covered with smiley-face suns. Ten of those sheets aren't yet blasted through with BB-gun pellets.

Leslie smiles the smile people use at funerals. "One of the

ways we build friendships is by answering questions. A good way to do this is through small talk. You respond with something cheery about your day or your family."

Room 14 is a morgue. Powder-blue walls and no window. Only the tick of the clock and the buzz and flicker of the fluorescent light remind me I'm still alive.

I slump down in my seat and cross my arms.

Socially maladaptive. According to the special-ed teacher, that's what I am. Sentenced to a semester in Leslie's "Sunshine Club," I'm one of the lucky ones up for parole at Christmas break.

I glance at the lifers. Ken and Kerry, autistic twins; Larry, who slugged a cook. Not sure how cramming in a tiny room for an hour after school will turn any of us into charmers.

The word *maladaptive* scrawled in invisible ink across my forehead just stole another hour of my life. Today, I don't have the time.

"I can see you're defensive, but look around you, Sam." Leslie's eyes plead. "These boys are here to be your friends."

Another snore from Bryan.

"Let's try a role-play. I'll pretend I like you." She perks up and clears her throat. "Remember, small talk. Answer with something general and light." Her smile widens, so do her eyes. "I'd love to hear something about your family."

I check the clock, look back at her, and nod. "My dad is dead. Don't worry about it, because he was a loser drunk who dug holes for a living. But he was generous. Kind enough to leave me this damn disease as my inheritance."

Leslie's smile is gone, her face frozen.

I push back from the table. "He left my mom for some other gal and then got himself killed." I stand. "And his replacement, Old Bill, is almost as bad. Any other questions?" I pick up my backpack and walk to the door. "Do appreciate the small-talk lesson."

Bryan's snore catches on something ugly, and he wakes with a "Huh!"

Before the door closes, a quieter Leslie goes to work on another victim. "You're quiet in group today, Bryan."

I jog to my locker, drop to the ground, and change into running shoes. I push through the front doors of Mitrista High. Outside, air hangs heavy, full of October mist. My lungs suck in the soup.

I stand and stretch and jog out of town. It's quiet. Birds, frogs, crickets—thick air smothers them all. The paved road ends and shoes hit gravel. My pace evens. My brain clears.

Shouldn't have come down on Leslie. Ain't her fault.

I jog through Bland—population sixteen—past three houses and Crusty's Coop, and reach tiny Pierce. It's only a minute's run from our farm on the near side of town to the Shell station here.

Two cars filling up? Today's 10K must be a bigger race than I thought.

Behind me, gravel pops and crackles, and I glance over my shoulder. Three school buses approach. I drift to the road's edge as they rumble by. A minute later, a string of twenty more overtakes me. I reluctantly fall in line behind them, and we all turn left into the Northwoods Wildlife Refuge.

The race won't start for an hour, but already a crowd gathers. I dash through the parking lot and join the onlookers beneath a string of colored pennants. I weave through the people until I reach the rope cordoning off the runners' starting area. The grassy field is littered with athletes from all over Minnesota, and above them stretches a large banner.

NORTHWOODS 10K OFF-ROAD CLASSIC

Kids wearing numbers small-talk easily. They laugh and stretch and check the sky.

I lean against the rope that separates me from them. I glance up, too. It will rain. It will rain hard and fast and their running shoes will stick in the mud. The sloppy path through the woods will make for a slow race. But it will be a race, and I don't have a number, and I'm on the wrong side of the rope.

A woman hands me a program with the list of runners. I scan the schools, the names. Over two hundred numbers today. I trace the list with my finger and locate the Cs. Sam Carrier would have been number thirty.

"Carrier?"

I look up. Coach Lovett approaches. Mitrista's new running coach weighs in at over three hundred pounds. But for an extra thousand a year, I guess a shop teacher will do most anything.

"From what I hear, you'd win this race. What's holdin' you

back, son?" I look over his shoulder at Mitrista's four entrants. Two shove each other; darn near a fistfight. Coach follows my gaze. "Lord knows we need ya." He turns back toward me. "Mailed you off a sports waiver. You get that signed?"

I exhale slow and kick at the dirt.

"Just need *one* of your folks' signatures," he says, and taps my shin with his shoe. Coach steps nearer and whispers. "Your stepdad never has to see it."

I blink hard, and my mouth gapes. Coach smiles.

"When I took this job from Coach Johnson, I asked him for the name of Mitrista's best runner. Don't you think that runner should be on the running team?"

"He told you about Old Bill?" I ask.

"Told me a lot of things about you. Didn't understand the half of them."

I stare down at the rope, feel the first drops of rain on the back of my neck, and nod. "Farm needs work, and he don't want me doin' extras. Besides, keepin' a secret from him ain't that easy."

Coach steps back. "Reckon not. But it's a shame to see all that speed go to waste. Think on it." He turns, takes one step back toward the team, and stops. "When it rains, that trail will be either grease or quicksand. Bad footing takes a runner down. Sure'd like to know where the slick spots are." He faces me, smiles, and leans forward. I lean in, too.

"How'd you like to give the trail a quick run? We could use a scouting report." He pats my back. "Don't need a waiver signed for that."

I straighten.

I'd be running for the team.

My hand clenches, crushes the program, and my shoulder leaps three times.

Coach takes off his cap, runs his hand through thinning hair. "What in the world is that?"

He saw. He asked. Coach Johnson must not have told him. Probably seconds until he takes back his offer. I lift the rope, duck under, and dart past him toward the trailhead.

The sky dims. Moments later, rain falls straight and hard. It lands with giant, soaking glops.

Runners dash for cover beneath the race tent. Spectators race to their cars. I stand and let water bounce off my jerking shoulder, stream off my sniffing nose. I'm in nearly constant motion. Today, like every day, seven seconds of still is all I get.

A megaphoned voice fights through the storm. "Due to weather conditions, the Northwoods 10K Classic is postponed! Race postponed!"

Whoops and groans go up from beneath the tent, and numbered kids streak back into the rain, hurdle the rope, and thunder toward waiting buses. I give my head a violent shake. I'm left alone.

Minutes pass, maybe more. Soaked cotton suctions onto my skin, but I don't want shelter. I want to feel the chill. I want to feel *something.* I spin around, watch raindrops dance in the puddles, and think how close I was to running a race.

I slosh into the starting area. The clearing is a small lake, and water licks my shoelaces. A number floats by. I scoop it up and put it on—stretch and smile like a numbered kid should. The downpour eases for a few seconds, and I can faintly make out where the course bottlenecks and disappears into the woods. With the tree cover from there on, it'd be a drier run.

In the first grouping, Sam Carrier. He holds the fastest time of any senior this year—

A splotch of red shifts against the trees. A figure stands near the entrance to the course.

I look around. Shadows mill about the tent, but that's all.

"Hey," I holler. "You probably didn't hear. They called it!"

The kid doesn't move.

I walk nearer. "You can't run this course in this rain. It washes out. Ten more minutes and they'll cancel it for today!" I squint toward the road. "Your team's probably waiting for you in the bus!"

I turn back. The guy in red is gone.

I blink hard and splash through the clearing.

Late afternoon with skies this dark? Kid'll get lost for sure.

"Hold up!" I dart in after him.

Can't be more than a few steps ahead.

I run my hard, angry run, but fifteen minutes pass and I haven't caught anyone. No way he's still in front of me. He probably never started in—

A flash of red rounds the next bend.

I push harder but don't gain.

Use your head, Carrier!

I duck onto a footpath that snakes through dense tree cover. Sticks and brambles crunch beneath my feet, and tree limbs gouge and scratch my arms. I pop out of the woods and rejoin the trail as the kid passes. He screams, startled, and races by me. It's not a boy scream.

Can't be.

I grit my teeth and pull alongside her on a straightaway through a field.

"What are you doin'?" I huff.

"I'm running a race." She speaks easily, her breath barely audible.

I'm quiet except for the squeak of my waterlogged shoes. I pick up my pace, glance to my left. Our arms bump and we reenter the woods.

"You know nobody else is?" I say.

"What?" she asks.

"Running a race."

She pulls up. I try to stop and turn, but my feet slide on a tree root. Both feet flip up, and I land on my gut in a puddle of mud. I groan, push up to my knees, and look up at her.

I watch raindrops trickle down her cheek; see them kiss her lips before continuing their path down her neck. The drops disappear behind the red shirt and shorts that cling tight against her, before they emerge and trail down her legs, drip off her body. *Lucky raindrops.*

Her body is beautiful and she runs fast and I can't remember who spoke last.

"Weren't you racing, too?" She looks at me, all of me. I wish I were covered with more mud. My opponent cocks her head, gently bites her lip.

I look down. "The sky is dark. I thought you might get lost."

She moves close. I glance up, but I'm still on my knees and I can't find an appropriate spot to put my gaze. I drop my eyes to her ankles.

Even her ankles are pretty.

"So you ran through the woods to make sure I'd stay on the trail?"

I nod.

She laughs. It's cute. "Where do you go to school?"

"Mitrista."

"Well, Mr. Mitrista, I run for Minnetonka, and I don't need your help. But I am training, and I do need these miles." She whispers, "Thanks for the push."

She reaches out her hand, but when I don't shake it, she brushes soaked hair off my forehead. My eyes close, and when I open them she's looking at her smeary brown fingers. She smiles and leans forward. Her breath is warm against my ear.

"You're muddy."

She straightens and takes off running.

I turn to watch. She stops and looks back over her shoulder. "Are you going to make it home?"

I nod my mud-caked head and point toward the ground. "I live here."

Again, she smiles.

I look down where my finger points at the mud puddle. *I live here? What kind of stupid line is that? And get up off your knees, Carrier!*

I grab a nearby limb and haul myself to my feet. "I meant that I live near here."

She's gone.

I glance around. My muscles don't jerk, and I close my eyes. I breathe deep, and like the third runner who finally catches up, the disease overtakes me. Slowly at first—a hard eyeblink. But that's not enough; there's more that has to work its way out, and my teeth grind. Movement spreads to my shoulder, and soon my whole body springs to twitchy life.

Good thing she ran off when she did.

I run through our imagined conversation start to finish.

"Hi, my name's Sam. What school do you run for? What's your name? Do you like muddy guys who talk to you from their knees?" I exhale long and hard. *Shouldn't have bolted out of that small-talk lesson.*

I stare one last time down the path where the most beautiful girl in the world had run. Then I take off my number, turn, and trudge back the way I came.